WICCA
YEAR OF MAGIC

FROM THE WHEEL OF
THE YEAR TO THE CYCLES OF THE MOON,
MAGIC FOR EVERY OCCASION

LISA CHAMBERLAIN

STERLING ETHOS
New York

STERLING ETHOS
New York

An Imprint of Sterling Publishing Co., Inc.

STERLING ETHOS and the distinctive Sterling Ethos logo
are registered trademarks of Sterling Publishing Co., Inc.

Originally published as *Wicca Wheel of the Year Magic* in 2017 and
Wicca Moon Magic in 2016 by Wicca Shorts.

This publication includes alternative therapies that have not been scientifically tested,
is intended for informational purposes only, and is not intended to provide or replace
conventional medical advice, treatment or diagnosis or be a substitute to consulting
with licensed medical or health-care providers. The publisher does not claim or
guarantee any benefits, healing, cure or any results in any respect and shall not be
liable or responsible for any use or application of any content in this publication in any
respect including without limitation any adverse effects, consequence, loss or damage
of any type resulting or arising from, directly or indirectly, any use or application of any
content herein. Any trademarks are the property of their respective owners, are used
for editorial purposes only, and the publisher makes no claim of ownership and shall
acquire no right, title or interest in such trademarks by virtue of this publication.

ISBN 978-1-4549-4109-5
ISBN 978-1-4549-4110-1 (e-book)

Distributed in Canada by Sterling Publishing Co., Inc.
c/o Canadian Manda Group, 664 Annette Street
Toronto, Ontario, Canada M6S 2C8
Distributed in the United Kingdom by GMC Distribution Services
Castle Place, 166 High Street, Lewes, East Sussex, England BN7 1XU
Distributed in Australia by NewSouth Books
University of New South Wales, Sydney, NSW 2052, Australia

For information about custom editions, special sales, and premium and corporate
purchases, please contact Sterling Special Sales at 800-805-5489
or specialsales@sterlingpublishing.com.

Manufactured in Canada

2 4 6 8 10 9 7 5 3 1

sterlingpublishing.com

Design by Gina Bonanno and Sharon Leigh Jacobs
Cover by Elizabeth Mihaltse Lindy
Picture credits—see page 164

FOR SALLY SUZANNE,

who sees the magic in each day

CONTENTS

PART ONE

THE WHEEL AT A GLANCE

PART TWO

DAYS OF POWER: THE SABBATS

PART THREE

MOON MAGIC

INTRODUCTION

THE ANCIENTS LIVED BY A FUNDAMENTAL TRUTH THAT IS often lost in our fast-paced world—that time is circular as much as it is linear. Their calendars were created by the cyclical movement of the Sun and the Moon, rather than the mathematical division of time into hours, weeks, or months. Following the Wheel of the Year by honoring the Sabbats and Esbats—the holidays of the Wiccan calendar—helps us integrate this concept of circular time into our daily lives. The Wheel provides a sense of rhythm to the year, as the equal increments of days and weeks between the Sabbats and Esbats allow us to feel the seasons and lunar cycles turning together in a beautiful dance.

The Sabbats also provide a context for honoring the dynamic relationship between the Goddess and the God. As the seasons turn, the divine pair shifts from mother and child to cocreative consorts and then back again. We honor these shifting roles and aspects throughout the year, with each Sabbat representing a point in the overarching story. This close participation with the cycles of the season is what some Wiccans refer to as "turning the Wheel."

Likewise, the Esbats keep us attuned to the rhythms of the Moon's ever-shifting cycles. The Moon is a vital presence in our world, with much to teach us about the eternal rhythms of the Universe, the powers of Nature, and the magical potential that is ours to tap into when we align our intentions with lunar energy. For millennia, the Moon has been associated with many central concerns of human existence: love, passion, fertility, mystery, death and rebirth, and the afterlife, just to name a few. It's no wonder that this celestial body is the domain of the Goddess!

This guide is intended to help you deepen your experience of the Wheel of the Year and grow in your magical practice. The practical elements are accessible enough for beginners, but those with more magical experience are still likely to find plenty of new information, ideas, and tips to enhance their journey.

In part one, we'll introduce the concepts inherent to the Wheel of the Year and its origins and development within traditional Wicca. Part two takes a closer look at each of the Sabbats—their significance within the context of the ever-changing seasons, the part they play in the changing relationships between the Goddess and the God, and the spiritual themes they ask us to reflect upon when we celebrate them.

You'll learn about the historical origins of each holiday and the associated traditions and practices that our European pagan ancestors have handed down over the centuries. You'll also find magical correspondences for spellwork and celebration of each Sabbat, as well as spells and other magical workings tailored specifically for each point on the Wheel.

Part three is devoted to understanding the power of the Moon, its relationship to the Esbats and the Triple Goddess, and the opportunities it provides for aligning your magic with its phases. We'll cover the lunar cycle in detail, chart the Moon's appearance in the sky as it moves through each phase, and identify the best approaches to magic at each stage of the cycle. The spells, recipes, and other hands-on information are all focused on lunar energies and accessible to beginners.

A dynamic, creative, and evolving approach to connecting with divine Nature is at the heart of Wicca and other forms of modern paganism. When you choose to mark the Sabbats and Esbats, you are participating in a timeless tradition of honoring the endless cycles of Nature and the divine workings of the Universe. May these pages support and inspire you, whether you're new to Wicca or a seasoned practitioner looking for new perspectives.

Blessed Be.

PART ONE

THE WHEEL AT A GLANCE

INVENTING THE WHEEL

IN THE DAYS BEFORE CLOCKS AND CALENDARS, PEOPLE MARKED the passage of time and the turning of the year by following the movements of the Sun and the stars. They didn't have months measured out in 30 or 31 days but instead followed the Moon as it cycled from New Moon to Full Moon and back to New Moon again.

It was Nature that told people what time it was, and they depended entirely on Nature's clock for their sustenance. A hard Winter, a weak harvest, or a decline in wild game could mean extreme misfortune and even death. It's no surprise that our ancestors regularly took time to pay homage to Nature, in the form of deities and spirits of the land, to express gratitude for their blessings and ask for assistance in the coming season.

The rituals and traditions used to mark the turning of the seasons in the ancient world varied widely across the globe and evolved over time. In the Western world, where Wicca finds its roots, there's a rich diversity of lore from the ancient Egyptians, Greeks, Romans, Celts, and Germanic peoples. These cultures worshipped different gods and goddesses and had different names for their holy days, but the dates on which their observations took place were generally consistent.

For example, in early February, the ancient Egyptians celebrated the Feast of Nut in honor of this mother goddess's birthday, while the Romans were busy with the purification and fertility rituals of Lupercalia, a holiday commemorating the mythical founders of Rome. The Celts also saw this as a time of purification as they celebrated Imbolc, and the Swedish Norse observed Dísablót, a time to honor the feminine spirits of the family (a tradition that lives on today in the annual fair known as the Disting). Many cultures practiced weather divination on this day. One custom of Germanic tribes has survived all the way into the present in the form of the North American holiday Groundhog Day.

Wicca was born out of a desire to reconnect with the spiritual practices of our ancestors—those who lived and worshipped in the old ways, before the Christianization of Europe (and much of the rest of the world). Inspired by the English occult revival of the late 1800s, Gerald Gardner and others set about reviving what they believed was an ancient pan-European religion, or "witch-cult," as one anthropologist described it, still surviving in hidden pockets of England and elsewhere.

An important aspect of the newly reconstructed "witchcraft," as Gardner and his coveners called it, was observing the old pagan holidays, or "Sabbats" as they came to be known. Gardner's new twentieth-century coven would meet on the days of these ancient festivals and enact special rituals to celebrate them. They also met at each Full Moon. These lunar ritual occasions are called Esbats, though the term can be used to describe any meeting of a coven that isn't a Sabbat celebration. You'll find more information about the Esbats on pages 118–119.

Gardner's coven marked only four Sabbats, celebrated on November 1, February 2, May 1, and August 1. These dates were based on the ancient Celtic calendar, which divided the year into a "dark half," or Winter (from Nov 1 to April 30) and a "light half," or Summer (from May 1 to October 31). In this system, which was based on agricultural cycles, the dates of February 2 and

August 1 mark the midpoints of each half of the year. These four dates are also recognized as the "cross-quarter" days of the solar year, as they fall roughly halfway between the solstices and equinoxes.

Gardner's coven would meet on the evening before the Sabbat day, a practice that aligned with the Celtic tradition of the new day beginning at sundown. Hence, these Sabbats as envisioned by Gardner were called November Eve, February Eve, and so on.

Other Pagan groups that emerged during this time, such as the Order of Bards, Ovates, and Druids, incorporated additional ancient sacred dates into their practices. For millennia, the Summer and Winter Solstices were of the utmost importance to the Norse and Anglo-Saxon peoples, and many cultures in Mesopotamia and elsewhere observed the Spring and Autumn Equinoxes. Neolithic structures throughout Ireland and the United Kingdom suggest that these astronomical occasions were significant to the predecessors of the Celts as well.

Gardner ultimately celebrated these solar holidays alongside the cross-quarter days, creating what we now know in Wicca as the eightfold Wheel of the Year. As Wicca evolved and spread, the Sabbat days took on more specific names, usually borrowed from the ancient cultures that celebrated them.

These names vary across traditions, but the most common ones in use today are a blend of Celtic, Norse, and Anglo-Saxon names: Yule, Imbolc, Ostara, Beltane, Litha, Lammas, Mabon, and

Samhain. Aidan Kelly, an influential American figure in Wicca and other modern forms of Paganism, is credited with coming up with this naming system in the late twentieth century.

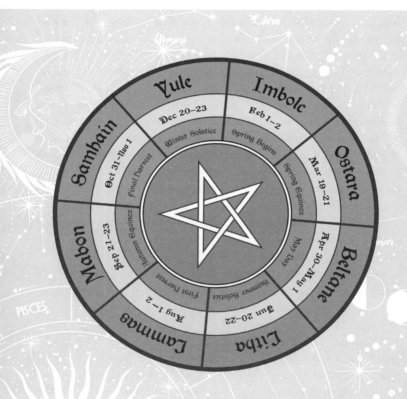

Note: If you live in the Southern Hemisphere, please see part two for the dates of each Sabbat in your area.

Since Gardner's day, we have learned much more about the original theory of the ancient pan-European religion—namely that there wasn't one. There are many similarities in various ancient practices across wide swaths of Europe because the Celts, Romans, and Germanic tribes conquered large territories and spread their traditions as they did so. But each region still maintained its distinct religious identity, making for a broad diversity of deities, beliefs, and customs. There's scant evidence that any one ancient civilization in Europe marked all eight of the modern Sabbats. Furthermore, the celebrations on these days would not have been only for the "witches" of the time. Instead, entire communities participated in rituals and festivities.

It is not historically accurate to describe the Wiccan Wheel of the Year as an exact revival of pre-Christian paganism. Nonetheless, it could be argued that as the Wheel evolved over the past several decades via the expansion of Wicca and other modern Pagan belief systems, we now have something that comes closer to a "pan-European witch-cult revival" than what Gardner could ever have envisioned. While the ritual component of Sabbat celebrations tends to be specific to Wicca—the honoring of the God and Goddess as viewed through a Wiccan framework—many practitioners observe additional customs that date back to antiquity. For example, the ancient tree-worshipping practice that involves dancing around a Maypole is a popular way to celebrate Beltane, while those who work with magical herbs might make a point of gathering some at Litha, when herbs are traditionally thought to be at their most potent.

Indeed, the wide range of practices we see today—whether passed down through the generations or discovered by historians and anthropologists—provides eclectic Wiccans and other Pagans with increasingly more information to work with as they create their own Sabbat celebrations.

A Timeless Cycle

In the twenty-first century, our day-to-day lives are mostly focused on the linear aspect of time, with our daily and weekly schedules, deadlines, countdowns to anticipated events, and perception of time as a limited resource. Ancient cultures, on the other hand, had a different orientation to time, viewing it as a never-ending circle.

The Celts understood this intrinsically, as you can see when examining just about any piece of Celtic artwork. The infinite looping of interweaving lines in the knots and crosses evokes a sense of creation without beginning or end. All who observed the regularly shifting patterns of the Sun's journey across the sky, from its southernmost point at the Winter Solstice to its northernmost point at the Summer Solstice and back again, would have experienced this same "loop."

Following the Wheel of the Year helps us integrate this concept of circular time into our lives. As we mark each Sabbat, we consciously witness the turning of each season in exquisite detail, honoring the cycles of life and death and those of growth and decay. It also helps us to be more present, as the steady flow of holidays to prepare for and celebrate keeps us from rushing headlong through the seasons with barely a passing glance at the natural world.

The Wheel also provides a sense of rhythm. The equal increments of days and weeks between the Sabbats help us anchor our sense of time passing in a beautiful symmetry. The eight-fold structure gives definition to a truth we've always subconsciously understood—that there are not four seasons but eight, as the "in-between" seasons bridge the gaps between the "cardinal" seasons of Winter, Spring, Summer, and Autumn.

This cyclical quality is also seen in the dynamic relationship between the Goddess and the God, each phase of which is represented by a different season. At the Winter Solstice, the Goddess gives birth to the God, and each Spring she is restored to her Maiden aspect as the two grow together. As Summer begins, they unite as lovers and the God impregnates the Goddess, ensuring that he will be born again after his death in late Autumn, when the Mother Goddess becomes the Crone.

Indeed, each deity is forever changing aspects—from young to old, from strong to weak, and from bountiful to barren. Both God and Goddess can manifest in more than one aspect at once: the Goddess is both Mother and Crone in the dark, cold months, and both Mother and Maiden in the early Spring. The God is a seed in the Goddess's womb even as he ages and dies at the end of the growing season.

As we recognize these shifting, overlapping aspects and the seasonal changes they represent, we become cocreative participants in the cycles of Nature. This is why many Wiccans refer to the honoring of the Sabbats as "turning the Wheel."

The Sabbats

Sabbats are known to many Wiccans as "days of power," since they occur at significant moments in the solar year: the solstices, the equinoxes, and the cross-quarter points in between, which is when Earth energies are at their height.

In many traditions, a distinction is made between "greater Sabbats" and "lesser Sabbats." The cross-quarter days are called the greater Sabbats because they fall at the points where the shifts between seasons are most palpable. Greater Sabbats are considered to be days of strong magical power. We also have the most detailed information about these holidays because we have information about the ancient pagan customs of the Greeks, the Romans, and the Celts.

Many modern Wiccan practices on these days are rooted in what we know about the ancient Irish, who were able to keep much of their early literature safe from destruction during the Dark Ages. This may be why the cross-quarters take their names largely from the Irish traditions: Imbolc (February 2), Beltane (May 1), and Samhain (October 31). The exception here is Lammas (August 1), whose name is Anglo-Saxon in origin, though many Wiccans and Pagans use the Irish name Lughnasa instead.

Less is known about the specific details of solstice and equinox celebrations, but what knowledge we do have is mostly rooted in ancient Norse and Anglo-Saxon cultures. Those living in the northern reaches of Europe would have observed the solstices, as they lived in regions where the differences in daylight over the course of the year are more stark than elsewhere on the continent.

The names for these solar Sabbats, as they are often called, are based less on history than the names of the cross-quarter days. Yule can be traced back to an actual pagan celebration on that date. The names for Ostara and Litha are related to ancient Norse culture, but they were not necessarily the names of holidays the Norse observed on those dates. Mabon is the most "invented" of all the Sabbat names, taken from a Welsh mythological figure loosely related to the mother–son archetype of the Goddess and the God.

Again, these names vary across Wiccan and other modern Pagan traditions. For example, people on the newly evolving path of Norse Wicca may use Norse names for all of the Sabbats. Those who align more with the Celts might decline to use the standard names for the solar holidays and simply refer to them as Summer Solstice, Autumn Equinox, and so on.

However, despite all the diversity in the names, customs, and practices that surround the Wheel of the Year, the traditions usually have a few things in common: feasting, ritual, and appreciation for the natural world in all of its beauty and abundance. For Wiccans who include spellwork in their practice, the energies surrounding the Sabbats make them excellent opportunities to work magic.

Turning the Wheel

Now that you've been introduced to the origins and development of the Wheel of the Year, it's time to delve more deeply into each of these powerful days on the Wiccan calendar.

In part two, we'll take a close look at each of the greater and lesser Sabbats. You'll learn a bit about the historical contexts from which these modern holidays have evolved and how these sacred days honor the cocreative relationship between the Goddess and the God. You'll also find tips and ideas for holding Sabbat celebrations, and a few suggested spells and other magical workings that correspond with the themes and season of each holiday.

Then, in part three, we'll dive deep into the mysterious energies of the Triple Moon Goddess and the infinite possibilities of lunar magic. If you keep a Book of Shadows, you might want to grab it now, since you're bound to find information that will help you plan your own magical Wheel of the Year!

PART TWO:

DAYS OF POWER:
THE SABBATS

OLD TRADITIONS MADE NEW

ONE KEY QUALITY OF WICCA THAT HAS FUELED ITS EXPANSION over the past several decades is its dynamic capacity for reinvention and reinterpretation. There is a basic framework in place for general beliefs and traditions, but there's no universally prescribed way to go about any of the rituals and practices, including Sabbat celebrations.

There are still lineage-based covens like those in the Gardnerian and Alexandrian traditions, whose members follow ritual protocols established early in Wicca's development. But even these groups are bound to alter at least some details, as each coven is a unique collection of individuals with their own understanding of the original Gardnerian material. In fact, those familiar with the history of Wicca will recognize that even Gardner revised and reworked his Book of Shadows.

As Wicca has grown and evolved, infinite variations on the older traditions have emerged. This is in large part due to eclectic practitioners, but it's also because creativity and invention are simply part of the experience of the Craft itself. Many people who identify as Wiccans and Witches today feel perfectly comfortable improvising and inventing rituals and other traditions for the Sabbats.

Although we'll cover general suggestions for observing each Sabbat, you won't find any instructions about what to do or say during your formal rituals in the following pages. (For those who would like help getting started with Wiccan ritual format, examples can be found in many sources in print and online. See "Suggestions for Further Reading" on pages 156–157 for some great places to start.) Instead, the focus here is on getting a solid sense of what each holiday is all about so you can develop your own approach to celebrating from a well-informed perspective.

In each section, we'll explore the seasonal context of the Sabbat and the associated themes that are often incorporated into Wiccan and other Pagan observances, including the stage it represents in the mythological relationship between the Goddess and God. We'll also take a brief tour of the pagan history behind each Sabbat—the myths, beliefs, and customs that have inspired our modern celebrations—and common ways in which these have been incorporated.

As for magic, you'll find two examples of spellwork in each section that are aligned with the seasonal and divine energies of the Sabbat. These can be followed as is or adapted to suit your style. They can also inspire more ideas about how to approach magical work on these days of power.

Preparing for Magical Sabbats

Whether you're celebrating solo or with a group of like-minded Witches, it can be fun to plan ahead for your Sabbats, gathering food, decorations, and ideas for making the most out of the upcoming holiday. As mentioned earlier, the diversity of Wiccan practice makes it difficult to generalize about what any given Sabbat celebration might look like. However, there are a few key elements that Sabbats tend to have in common: fire, feasting, and an altar with sacred items and Sabbat decorations.

Sabbats are a time to honor the divine energies of Nature and connect with the timeless traditions of our pagan ancestors. For the ancients, most of these sacred occasions were fire festivals, honoring the Sun's role in sustaining life. Bonfires, torches, and associated fire rituals played a central role in the celebrations, and some of these traditions are still practiced to this day. Fire is indeed a potent part of magic, representing light and transformation, and should be part of your Sabbat activities whether or not any spellwork is involved—even if it's just in the form of a few candles on your altar.

Another component of Sabbat festivities that connects us to our ancestors is the act of preparing and enjoying a feast. The transformation of raw materials, such as vegetables, grains, and meat, into a delicious meal is its own kind of magical cocreation with the Universe. For solitary practitioners, a "feast" may be a little harder to pull off, but this word doesn't have to be taken literally. Whether you cook yourself a nice meal or simply enjoy a healthy snack, just be sure to treat yourself to some nourishment from Nature at this time.

Setting up your altar for a Sabbat is a wonderful way to get into the spirit of a holiday. Whether you have a full-time altar or sacred space, or spruce up an end table, it's hardly a Sabbat without special decorations. Suggestions for seasonally appropriate foods and altar decorations are included in the Correspondences in each section.

If you can, start setting up a day or two before the Sabbat. If this isn't possible, you can still start gathering the items you'll put on the altar when the time comes—seasonal symbols, altar cloths, corresponding candles, flowers, herbs*, and crystals. The altar is the focal point for your Sabbat ritual, so the more attention you put into it, the more receptive your connection with the God and Goddess will be. It doesn't matter whether your altar is simple or elaborate—it's the energy with which you put it together that matters.

Because Sabbats can be a time for affirming our power to cocreate our reality through magic, Witches often incorporate magic and spellcraft into their Sabbat celebrations. You can plan a successful, magical Sabbat by identifying in advance the magical goal(s) you'd like to work on. Then gather your items and have your spell instructions ready to go for when your ritual begins.

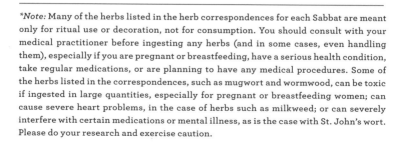

Note: Many of the herbs listed in the herb correspondences for each Sabbat are meant only for ritual use or decoration, not for consumption. You should consult with your medical practitioner before ingesting any herbs (and in some cases, even handling them), especially if you are pregnant or breastfeeding, have a serious health condition, take regular medications, or are planning to have any medical procedures. Some of the herbs listed in the correspondences, such as mugwort and wormwood, can be toxic if ingested in large quantities, especially for pregnant or breastfeeding women; can cause severe heart problems, in the case of herbs such as milkweed; or can severely interfere with certain medications or mental illness, as is the case with St. John's wort. Please do your research and exercise caution.

A Note on Dates

The calendar dates given in this guide are the most commonly cited, but the actual dates on which these holidays are observed can vary for a few reasons.

When it comes to the solar (or lesser) Sabbats, the exact moment of each solstice and equinox varies from year to year due to a slight misalignment between the Gregorian calendar and the rate at which the Earth rotates around the Sun. Furthermore, the dates for these solar events are typically identified using coordinated universal time (UTC). This means that depending on where you live, a given solstice or equinox may occur one day before or one day after the official date of the event. For this reason, a range of dates is provided for these holidays. You can consult a calendar to find out which dates they fall on in a given year in your area.

For cross-quarter (or greater) Sabbats, some sources give the day before. For example, Imbolc might be listed as February 1 instead of February 2. This is in keeping with Celtic tradition, which marks the beginning of the day at sundown. You will see both dates in this guide.

Finally, for those living in the Southern Hemisphere, the dates of the Sabbats are completely reversed, so Yule falls in June and Litha in December, and so on. These dates are also noted.

Some Wiccans, rather than following the modern calendar, use the movements of the Sun or the Moon to determine their cross-quarter day celebrations. A cross-quarter day is the halfway point between the two adjoining solar days—for example, Samhain marks the midpoint between the Autumn Equinox and the Winter Solstice. Samhain is commonly celebrated on October 31, but because the actual midpoint usually occurs closer to November 6 or 7, some covens and individuals may hold their Samhain celebrations then. Others may observe it on the first New Moon of the month or the first New Moon of the Zodiac sign in which the cross-quarter day falls. Because there's a lot of variance in when the midpoint falls from year to year, these alternate dates are not cited in the guide, but that doesn't mean you can't follow one of these systems if it resonates with you.

No matter which day you celebrate your Sabbat, just be sure to approach it with joy and reverence for the natural world, the Goddess and God who create and sustain life, and the beauty of the cycle of life and death that keeps the Wheel forever turning.

═ Y U L E ═

WINTER SOLSTICE

NORTHERN HEMISPHERE DATES:
DECEMBER 20-23

SOUTHERN HEMISPHERE DATES:
JUNE 20-22

PRONUNCIATION: *yool*

THEMES: Rebirth, quiet introspection, new year, hope, setting intentions, celebration of light

ALSO KNOWN AS: Winter Solstice, Midwinter, Alban Arthuan, Saturnalia, Yuletide

Celebrated on the date of the Winter Solstice, Yule is the point on the Wheel of the Year when we acknowledge the return of light. The nights have reached their longest point, creating a sense of darkness that is almost overbearing. The air is cold, the deciduous trees are completely bare, and for those in northern climates, the season of snow is in full swing.

Yet as far as the Sun is concerned, this is a turning point. The longest night is behind us, and the Sun will stay with us later each day, rising ever higher in the sky until the Summer Solstice, the turning point on the opposite side of the Wheel. There is the promise that the warmth of the growing season will eventually return.

However, it will be a few weeks before the changes are noticeable, as the increase in daylight is gradual. The Sun does not appear to alter its path across the sky during the days around the Winter Solstice. In fact, the word *solstice* comes from a Latin phrase meaning "sun standing." Much of Nature seems to be still at this point. Birds have migrated south, many animals are hibernating, and the snow covering the ground seems to have quieted the landscape. This is a time of turning inward, hunkering down, and tuning in to our deepest selves.

Many people see these short days and long nights as a time of self-reflection, spiritual study, and intention-setting for the coming year. But before the deep Winter sets in, we gather with friends and family to celebrate the renewal of the Sun and the hope that comes with emerging from the darkness. This has always been a traditional time for both spiritual observance and merriment, and it still is today, as we can see in the many different holidays and festivities associated with the start of the winter season.

In many Wiccan traditions, Yule is the start of the new year. The seasons of the Wheel and the annual story of the God and the Goddess have completed the circle and now begin again. The Goddess gives birth to the God, fulfilling the intention the divine pair set when they coupled at Beltane. As the Sun God, his symbolic death and return to the underworld at Samhain led to the darkness of the past six weeks, and now his rebirth brings back the light. The Goddess has transformed once again from her Crone aspect back to the Mother, who will now rest awhile from her labor and emerge rejuvenated in the Spring.

This segment of the mythological cycle is central to the Wiccan understanding of reincarnation—after death comes rebirth into new life. The Sun illustrates this truth through its cyclical disappearance and reappearance. The Earth, which never disappears, represents the never-ending presence of the divine Universe.

Winter Magic and Merriment

Of all the solar Sabbats, Yule is probably the one most clearly rooted in an ancient pagan holiday, as it takes its name from a festival celebrated in Germanic and Scandinavian cultures around the time of the Solstice. The original observance of Yule likely lasted for several days.

Many other ancient peoples also observed the Winter Solstice, as we can see by the number of Neolithic monuments—like Newgrange in Ireland—built to align with the sunrise on this day. The Romans celebrated Saturnalia around this time, which involved feasting and exchanging gifts as well as ritual sacrifice. In Persia, worshippers of the god Mithra celebrated his birth. The Druids of the Celtic Isles are said to have gathered sacred mistletoe and sacrificed cattle on the Winter Solstice.

While some forms of Wicca may base their Yule celebrations on some of these other regional traditions, the Norse and Anglo-Saxon customs that give this Sabbat its name are what the day is best known for. In the lands of Northern Europe, the Solstice festivities were the last opportunity for most people to socialize before the deep winter snows prevented travel. Germanic tribes held great gatherings, where feasting, drinking, and ritual sacrifice of livestock took place. Revelers lit bonfires and toasted

THE YULE LOG

to Norse gods such as Odin and Thor. These activities helped ensure a prosperous growing season in the coming new year. Some of the traditions observed during these ancient festivals— such as burning a Yule log, decorating with evergreen boughs and branches, enjoying wassail (a term for warm alcoholic beverages such as mulled cider or wine) and group singing—continued on through the centuries and are still part of many Christmas celebrations today.

The Yule log in particular was widespread in Europe, with many different regional customs attached to it. Traditionally made from a large log of oak, it was decorated with pine boughs, holly, or other evergreen branches and doused with cider or ale before being lit at the start of the festivities. In many places, this fire was lit with a piece of wood saved from the previous year's Yule log. The log was supposed to be harvested from the land of the household or received as a gift—to purchase it was deemed unlucky. The Yule fire was tended so that it didn't burn out on its own, in part to save a piece of the log to start the following year's fire. The length of time for the fire to burn varied, but was usually between 12 hours and 12 days.

The Yule festivities—caroling, games, the gift exchanges—took place around the warmth of the fire. In some places, the ashes from the Yule fire were used to make magical charms, sprinkled over the fields to encourage crops, or tossed into wells to purify the water. As with so many other pagan festivals, we can see that the magical power of fire was alive and well at Yule!

The most obviously pagan remnant surviving in today's holiday traditions is the use of mistletoe. This parasitic plant (called so because it attaches to a host plant, usually oak or apple trees) was significant to the Norse, the Celts, and the ancient Greeks and Romans. The significance of mistletoe at the Winter Solstice likely comes from the Druids, who viewed the plant's ability to stay green while the oak it grew on was without leaves as a sign of its sacred powers. Mistletoe was ritually harvested at this time with a golden sickle and fed to the animals to ensure fertility. It was also valued for its protective properties, particularly against fire and lightning, and was used in medieval times for healing. Once Christianity became more widespread, mistletoe was prohibited as a decoration, most likely due to its association with magic. It's not clear why "kissing under the mistletoe" became a tradition, but it's thought to have come from an ancient Norse myth involving the goddess Frigg and the death of her son Balder from an arrow made of mistletoe; when he was resurrected by the gods, Frigg joyfully proclaimed mistletoe to be a symbol of love and that she would kiss anyone who stood beneath the plant.

Celebrating Yule

Many covens meet just before dawn on the day of the Solstice to hold their Yule rituals and then watch the rebirth of the God enacted as the Sun rises. In some traditions, fires and candles are lit to encourage the Sun God's emergence, welcoming his returning light. The themes of the ritual may include regeneration, light in the darkness, and setting intentions for the new year.

In some Wiccan traditions, this is the time to ritually reenact the battle between the Oak King and the Holly King. These twin brothers represent the opposing poles of the Sun's annual journey through the seasons. The Holly King, representing the dark half of the year, reigns until the Winter Solstice, when he is cut down by the Oak King, who heralds the beginning of increased daylight. This story serves as a reminder that light and dark are both essential parts of existence in Nature—neither can exist without the other.

For solitary Wiccans who live "double lives" as far as mainstream society is concerned, Yule can be a challenging Sabbat to make time for, as so many are swamped with the obligations of the Christmas season. However, since plenty of the traditions associated with both holidays overlap, it's easy enough to infuse more conventional practices with a little Yule magic. For example, hang a sprig of holly above your door to ensure protection and good fortune for your family and your guests. Magically charge your Christmas tree ornaments before placing them on the branches. Whisper an incantation to the Goddess over cookies, spiced cider, or any other holiday goods you make for your friends, family, or coworkers.

You can spread the blessings of Yule throughout your community without anyone even knowing it!

For those without indoor hearths, a Yule log can be fashioned from a small tree branch—flatten it on one side so it will sit evenly on the altar and drill small holes to place candles into. Make sure to not leave any lit candles unattended, especially if you are placing them in wood. Go outside

and gather boughs of fir, juniper, or cedar, as well as pinecones, holly berries, and any other "natural decor" to bring the energies of protection, prosperity, and renewal into your home. (Note that holly berries should be kept out of reach of children and pets, as they can cause severe gastrointestinal issues if eaten.)

Use mistletoe to bring peace and healing to your life by placing leaves in a sachet or hanging it over your door. Honor the rebirth of the Sun by inscribing discs, pinwheels, or other solar symbols into a large red, orange, or yellow pillar candle. Light it at dawn on the day of the Winter Solstice to welcome the Sun and the new beginning of the Wheel of the Year.

Yule Correspondences

COLORS: Red, green, gold, silver, white, orange

CRYSTALS: Bloodstone, garnet, emerald, diamond, ruby, clear quartz

HERBS: Bayberry, blessed thistle, frankincense, chamomile, mistletoe, ivy, rosemary, all evergreens, oak and holly trees

FLOWERS: Sunflowers, dried flowers from Summer

INCENSE: Frankincense, cedar, juniper, pine, cinnamon, myrrh, bayberry

ALTAR DECORATIONS/SYMBOLS: Candles, evergreen wreaths and boughs, holly, mistletoe, pinecones, Yule log, snowflakes, pinwheels, yellow discs or other solar symbols and imagery

FOODS: Fruits, nuts, baked goods, cider, spiced cider, eggnog, ginger tea, wassail

INNER LIGHT MEDITATION

No matter which holidays you observe in December, it's hard to avoid the noise and bustle of the season. The commercialism of mainstream society is at its height, there are many social gatherings to attend, and everything seems to feel busier. It can be a struggle to stay balanced and grounded at this time, especially for people who are strongly affected by the lack of sunlight at this point in the year.

This simple visualization can help you connect with your inner light, where your connection to the divine resides. Meditation is very helpful for people from all walks of life. For Witches, it's a key tool for cultivating a magical state of mind. Here, the candle is a physical symbol for what you're connecting to on the ethereal plane: your inner flame. Adding a little greenery to the scene, even if it's just a few pine needles, brings in the grounding influence of the Earth element as well, but it's not strictly necessary for the meditation.

YOU WILL NEED

Small branch or bough from an evergreen tree,
such as pine or cedar (optional)

1 white votive candle

INSTRUCTIONS

Arrange the evergreen branches on your altar in a visually pleasing manner. Light the candle and sit quietly, gazing at the flame for a few moments. Then gently close your eyes. See the flame as a white light spreading from the center of your heart throughout the rest of your body. Hold this visualization and breathe deeply and slowly. If you find your mind drifting, gently return your focus to the white light suffusing your entire being. After 5 to 10 minutes, allow the light to relax back into the form of a candle flame sitting in the center of your heart. When you feel ready, open your eyes. All is well.

MAGICAL YULE BREW

This delicious tea is a nice nonalcoholic alternative to traditional wassail, though you can turn it into a hot toddy by adding whiskey, brandy, or vodka. Wassail played a part in ancient Norse fertility magic. It was poured onto the ground at Midwinter to encourage abundant crops to grow in the coming year.

To turn this tea into a magical brew, be sure to charge all ingredients before making it and to say a blessing as you pour the water over the tea and herb mixture. Then drink it in advance of (or during) ritual or spellwork. This recipe makes one cup, but you can adapt it to serve more. Just add one teabag, one lemon slice and one cinnamon stick to each additional serving and increase the rest of the ingredients as you see fit.

If you don't have muslin bag or cheesecloth to keep the herbs and spices in while steeping, you can let them float loose in the pot and use a strainer when pouring the tea into mugs. If you don't have a teapot, use a large mug or bowl and cover it with a plate while the tea is steeping.

═ YOU WILL NEED ═

½ teaspoon dried chamomile

¼ teaspoon allspice berries

Pinch grated ginger

⅛ teaspoon orange zest

Muslin bag or square piece of cheesecloth and kitchen twine (optional)

1 black tea teabag

1 cup (240 ml) hot water

1 lemon slice

5 whole cloves

Honey to taste

1 cinnamon stick

≡ INSTRUCTIONS ≡

Place the herbs and spices except for the lemon, cloves, and cinnamon stick into a muslin bag or cheesecloth, using the kitchen twine to secure the opening. Place this sachet into the teapot along with the teabag. Pour the hot water over the tea and herbs and cover, letting the tea steep for 3–5 minutes. Meanwhile, stud the lemon slice with the cloves. Pour the steeped tea into a mug and add the studded lemon slice. Sweeten with honey and stir with the cinnamon stick.

≡ IMBOLC ≡

PRONUNCIATION: *IM-bulk, IM-molg,* or *imb-OLC*

THEMES: Quickening, hope, renewal, fertility, purification, hearth and home, return of the light

ALSO KNOWN AS: Brigid's Day, Oimelc, Feast of Torches, Feast of Pan, Lupercalia, Snowdrop Festival, Feast of the Waxing Light

Although the Spring Equinox is our modern designation for the official beginning of Spring, it was Imbolc that traditionally marked the end of Winter in the pagan world.

As the midpoint of the dark half of the year, which begins with Samhain and ends at Beltane, Imbolc marks the time when the grip of Winter begins to soften and the Earth starts to come back to life. For people who live in northern climates, where snow and ice dominate the landscape, this is truly a celebration of hope and possibility, as the light grows stronger each day, and subtle signs of the coming of Spring begin to emerge.

The days are noticeably lengthening now, as the Sun God's power begins to grow. Among different Wiccan traditions, he is described variously as an infant nursing at the Goddess's breast and as a young boy making his way toward maturity. Either way, he is a waxing presence in the sky, higher and more visible with each passing day.

The Goddess, in the form of the Earth, is stirring from her rest following the birth of the God. We see this manifesting as the frozen ground begins to thaw, crocuses and daffodils poke through the surface, and the first birds pass through on their return migration from the southern climates. This is the time when the three-fold aspect of the Goddess shifts from Crone back into Maiden, as the air takes on a hint of youthful energy in the anticipation of warmer days just around the corner. Our ancestors paid close attention to these early signs of Spring. In the earliest days, these signs—for example, the blooming of the blackthorns—would have determined the date of festival.

The cross-quarter day was a time for weather divination in many cultures. In Celtic lore, the divine hag Cailleach, who would come out to gather the last of her firewood, determined the length of the Winter. If she wanted to make the Winter last awhile longer, she would make bright, sunny weather on Imbolc so she would enjoy a long day of gathering plenty of wood. If she slept through the day, the weather would be gloomy and cold, and the people would know that Winter was nearly over.

A Scottish tradition held that the serpent belonging to the goddess Brighid emerged from under the Earth on Imbolc to test the weather. If it remained aboveground, the Winter would end soon, but if it returned to its home, another month or more of cold weather was in store. Germanic tribes followed a similar custom with bears and badgers, which in later centuries was adapted to the groundhog and its shadow on Groundhog Day in the United States and Canada.

Imbolc also marks the beginning of the agricultural season, as it is the time when farmers ready the soil for the first planting and herd animals prepare to give birth. Farmers make needed repairs to their equipment before the season starts in earnest, and rituals for blessing tools and seeds are held at this time—a tradition going back for centuries, if not longer. In every aspect of life—for humans, animals and plants—Imbolc is the time to start moving around again after the long Winter's rest.

The name of this Sabbat comes from the ancient Irish and has been translated as "in the belly," referring to the pregnancy of ewes. A related name for the holiday is Oimelc, meaning "ewe's milk," though modern Pagans seem to use this name more so than the ancient Celts. These milk-producing livestock were crucial for survival for rural people in premodern times, especially at this point in the Winter when food stores might be running low or completely empty. For this reason, the onset of lambing season was an occasion for celebration!

Purification is another central focus at Imbolc, stemming from the oldest days when dwellings had to be shut tight against the cold for months and bathing was a very infrequent activity. The first sign of thaw meant it was time to throw open the doors; cleanse the house of the stuffy, stale air; and jump into the nearest body of water (once the ice had thawed, of course!). Sunlight was also a purifying force—a manifestation of the Element of Fire—and was taken advantage of as much as possible for renewing the body and the spirit.

Brighid, Goddess of Fire

Although each of the cross-quarter days has Celtic roots, Imbolc may be the most Celtic-influenced of the Wiccan Sabbats. While it's true that some forms of Wicca take their inspiration for this holiday from other peoples of pre-Christian Europe, such as the Greeks or the Norse, the most widely used name for the holiday is still Imbolc (or Imbolg, in some areas).

The celebration of Imbolc in Ireland, Scotland, and the Isle of Man goes back into prewritten history, and some of the earliest surviving Irish literature mentions this feast. The significance of the cross-quarter day may even predate the Celts themselves. Some of the Neolithic monuments in Ireland are aligned such that the Sun lights up their inner chambers on this day.

Many Wiccans borrow more than just the name of the Sabbat from the Celts. They also honor Brighid, who was traditionally the central focus of Imbolc celebrations in Celtic lands. Like the Wiccan Goddess, Brighid is a threefold, or triune, goddess with aspects that align with the Maiden, Mother, and Crone archetypes. In Irish mythology, she rules the three areas of smithcraft, healing, and poetry, all of which were powerful activities in Celtic culture.

As a healer, Brighid is associated with many springs and holy wells that were known for their healing and purifying properties. Her cauldron of inspiration sustained poets and bards, and her cocreative powers extended to midwifery and crafting.

Her rule over smithcraft, or metalworking—the alchemical art of transforming raw materials into weaponry and tools—is part of her association with the Element of Fire. She is said to have been born at sunrise, with a tower of flame bursting from her head and reaching all the way to heaven. She is called "keeper of the sacred flame," and in pre-Christian times her priestesses kept a perpetual fire in her honor at a temple in Kildare, Ireland.

Brighid is also considered the guardian of home and hearth and was invoked to protect livestock herds and assist in providing a fruitful harvest. She was associated with the cow, a symbol of motherhood and life sustenance, as well as with the light half of the year. As a result, her presence at this time in late Winter was very important to the people.

On Imbolc Eve, Brighid was believed to visit the households of those who invited her and bestow blessings on the inhabitants. Various customs for inviting her were practiced throughout the lands where she was worshipped. The most common included making her a bed out of a basket with white bedding and creating a straw doll-like figure of Brighid (called a Brídeóg). These corn dollies, as they are also called, were carried from door to door so each household could offer a gift to the goddess. Families would also enjoy a special meal and save some of the food and drink to leave outside for Brighid, along with clothing or strips of cloth for her to bless. The following morning, the family would inspect the ashes of their smoored fire for any marks that showed Brighid had indeed entered the house. The cloth would be brought back inside, now imbued with healing and protective powers.

Some people made "Brighid's crosses" from stalks of wheat that they formed into a square, an equilateral cross, or an ancient protection symbol resembling a counterclockwise swastika that was found in various cultures throughout the ancient world. These were hung over the entrances of homes and stables to protect the household from fire, lightning, and any threat to the animals and the harvest. The crosses would be left hanging throughout the year, until the following Imbolc, and are still used in some places today.

Brighid was such a central part of Irish pagan culture that she remained in the people's consciousness during the Christianization of the country. Imbolc is known throughout Ireland as Brighid's Day, as it is also the feast day of St. Brigid, one of Ireland's patron saints. There has been much debate about whether St. Brigid was a real-life abbess who lived in fifth-century Ireland or whether she is simply a Christianization of the goddess. Either way, people in Ireland tend to speak of the two Brighids as if they are one and the same.

Elements of this cross-quarter day were incorporated in Candlemas, a Christian holy day that involved the making and blessing of candles for the coming year. Many Wiccans and other Pagans with less specifically Celtic leanings also use the name Candlemas for this Sabbat.

Celebrating Imbolc

Fire plays a big role in most Wiccan Imbolc traditions. At coven celebrations, a high priestess may wear a crown of lit candles or carry tapers during ritual. This is done in honor of the Goddess stepping into her Maiden aspect and the God's growth into boyhood. Many practitioners light candles in each room of the house to welcome the Sun. They hold bonfires if the weather is fair and burn any evergreen decorations from the Yule Sabbat as a way of letting go of the past season, or even the past year.

For Wiccans, Brighid's status as a Fire goddess makes her an appropriate deity to recognize on a Sabbat that celebrates the return of the Sun. You can honor her in a variety of ways—by visiting a natural spring or holy well and making offerings, cleaning and purifying your home, lighting candles for her at your altar, or even engaging in writing or other creative activities. Try making a Brídeóg to place on your altar, and make Brighid's bed for her to rest in. If you made a Corn Mother for Lammas last year (see page 87), you can repurpose it, dressing her this time in white, yellow, or pink (think "Maiden" colors). The bed can be a small basket, a wooden box, or even a well-decorated shoebox. Just be sure to make it comfortable and attractive, with blankets and flowers, ribbons, and other decorations. Place your Brídeóg in the bed near your hearth (or altar, if you don't have a fireplace). Some leave a small wand for her, so she can use it to bless your home. You can also make your own Brighid's cross to hang over your doorway. Instructions for these Imbolc crafts can be easily found online or in other print sources.

Other traditional Imbolc activities include going for walks or hikes to look for signs of Spring in the surrounding countryside, taking a ritual bath for physical and energetic purification, and decorating and blessing farm equipment (such as ploughs) for the coming season. Placing a besom, or ritual broom, by the front door symbolizes sweeping out the stale energy of Winter and allowing fresh energy to enter your home and your life.

As with all cross-quarter Sabbats, a special feast is a great idea, particularly on February 1, or "Imbolc Eve." Bringing food to those in need after the long Winter—such as homeless shelters and elderly shut-ins—is an excellent way to raise abundance energy for your community.

Finally, Imbolc is a good time to perform self-dedication rituals or to undergo coven initiation if you are in a position to do so.

Imbolc Correspondences

COLORS: Red, white, yellow, pink

STONES: Garnet, ruby, onyx, bloodstone, amethyst

HERBS: Angelica, basil, bay leaf, myrrh, coltsfoot, heather

FLOWERS: Snowdrops, violets, crocus, daffodils, forsythia

INCENSE: Myrrh, cinnamon, violet, wisteria, jasmine, vanilla

ALTAR DECORATIONS/SYMBOLS: White flowers, potted bulbs, Brighid's cross, Brídeóg, sheep, cows, ploughs, cauldron, poems or poetry book, candles, or candle wheel

FOODS: Pumpkin and sunflower seeds, poppy seed pastries, dairy products, early spring vegetables

HEARTH AND HOME PURIFICATION RITUAL

You don't have to be a Witch to notice that the energy and mood of a home is always improved by a thorough cleaning, but making a magical experience out of it takes it to a whole new level. If you need to do this cleaning in stages, start a couple of days ahead of time, then put the finishing touches on your cleaning job right before the ritual.

1 blue candle

Bowl of water

Rosemary essential oil, or fresh or dried rosemary

Smudge stick of sage and lavender or sweetgrass

=== INSTRUCTIONS ===

First, clean your house from top to bottom. This includes the kitchen, which is the modern-day "hearth" for people who don't have working fireplaces in their homes. Clear away any cobwebs lurking in neglected corners, dust and wipe down all surfaces, sweep, mop, and vacuum. For best results, use all-natural cleaning agents made with essential oils, rather than chemical products. Be sure to give extra attention to any ritual or magical objects such as your altar, tools, and crystals. If you've been hanging on to any charms or other magical crafts that have finished serving their purpose, now is a good time to respectfully dispose of them. If weather permits, keep a window open or a door cracked while you clean, and be sure to listen to music that puts you in a happy mood.

When the house is ready, light the candle. Add 3 drops of rosemary essential oil to the water (or sprinkle in a pinch of fresh or dried rosemary) and say the following (or similar) words:

"I give thanks to the purifying essence of Fire.
I give thanks to the purifying essence of Water.
I call on them to bless and protect this home.
So let it be."

Place the blessed water in front of the candle.

Light the smudge stick and carry it through each room in the house. Walk in a clockwise motion, wafting the smoke into every corner. Open the doors and windows as much as possible, and be sure to keep the front door open for at least a few minutes after the smudging. (This allows any unwanted energy to exit your home.)

Finally, sprinkle a few drops of the rosemary water over the windowsills and doorways in each room. The candle can be left to burn out on its own, under supervision, or snuffed and lit again later for ordinary uses.

IMBOLC SEED AND CANDLE SPELL

This spell draws on the symbolic power of seeds at the center of the "hearth" that you create using three candles. The candles represent the three-fold aspect of Brighid, but calling on her directly for assistance isn't required. (If you feel a connection with her, then by all means ask!) Use this spell to set the tone for the coming growing season in the realms of creativity, healing, and abundance.

To prepare, spend some time identifying your goals. You might have three separate goals, such as finding new ideas and energy for a creative project; addressing a physical or emotional injury; and securing a new home. Or, you may have one goal that can be related to each of these domains in some way. You may want to do some journaling or meditating to help you clarify what you want to manifest at this time. If possible, take a ritual bath before working this spell.

As always, feel free to tailor the words to suit your own style and beliefs.

=== **YOU WILL NEED** ===

1 yellow Goddess candle

1 red God candle

Small handful (or a seed packet) of basil, pumpkin, or sunflower seeds

Small ceramic, stone, glass, or wooden bowl

3 white spell candles or tea lights

=== **INSTRUCTIONS** ===

Set up your altar with Imbolc-themed items and imagery. When you're ready to start, light the Goddess candle and say:

"I welcome and give thanks to the awakening Earth."

Light the God candle and say:

"I welcome and give thanks to the strengthening Sun."

Place the seeds into the bowl (if they're in a packet, pour them out). Hold the bowl in your hands for a moment. Visualize sending your personal power into each seed. See the bowl filling with light in your mind's eye. Raise the bowl toward the sky and charge the seeds with your voice by saying:

"Through these seeds of the Earth will come many blessings."

Now place the bowl on the altar and arrange the three white candles around it in a triangle shape. The candle at the top of the triangle represents inspiration. The bottom right candle is for healing, and the bottom left for abundance.

Light the top candle and say:

> *"By the power of the word, I am inspired to right action."*

Light the right-hand candle and say:

> *"By the healing waters of the well, I am purified."*

Light the left-hand candle and say:

> *"By the fire of the forge, I create my abundance."*

Now spend a few moments gazing upon your work. Give thanks again to the Goddess and the God. If you like, seal your spell with the words *It is done* or *Blessed Be*.

Leave the bowl in place until the candles have burned all the way down. Save the seeds for planting when it's appropriate to do so. You can also include them in any kind of abundance charm or sachet, or scatter them over the Earth outside of your home.

═ OSTARA ═

SPRING EQUINOX

NORTHERN HEMISPHERE DATES:
MARCH 19-21

SOUTHERN HEMISPHERE DATES:
SEPTEMBER 21-23

PRONUNCIATION: *OH-star-ah*

THEMES: Balance, renewal, action, beginnings, hope, new possibilities

ALSO KNOWN AS: Alban Eiler, Rites of Spring, Eostra's Day, Vernal Equinox, March Equinox, Spring Equinox, Lady Day, Bacchanalia

As the first solar Sabbat of the calendar year, Ostara marks the Spring Equinox, one of two points in the Sun's journey at which day and night are of equal length.

The Sun has crossed the "celestial equator" and will shine on Earth for longer each day until it reaches its zenith at the Summer Solstice. For Earth's inhabitants, this is a fortuitous moment, as the scarcity of Winter comes to an end and the growing season begins in earnest. On the modern calendar, this is the first day of Spring.

Depending on where you live, there may still be snow on the ground, but the Earth is beginning to thaw and rivers rise and overflow their banks. Green grass and spring flowers emerge; lambs, rabbits and chicks are born; and the promise of new life is felt on the breeze, which is milder than it was just a few weeks ago.

The waxing light is truly felt now, as the Sun's power seems to quicken. The lengthening of the days, first perceived at Imbolc, seem to grow at an even faster rate as the Sun sets later and further north with each passing day. But on Ostara, the light and the dark exist in equal measure, and this gives the holiday its primary theme of balance.

This balance is observed not only between night and day, but also in weather patterns—the harsh, bitter cold of Winter is behind us, yet the relentless heat of Summer has yet to arrive. In colder climates, it's not unusual for Spring and Winter to take turns during these days, with one day feeling more like February and the next more like May. Nonetheless, the fertility of the Earth becomes more and more undeniable as the slow energies of Winter give way to the fresh new vibrancy of Spring.

This is a time to reunite with the Earth in a tactile way after many months spent largely indoors. Gardeners may prepare soil and set seed trays out in the sunlight to sprout. Those who practice green Witchcraft may perform seed-blessing rituals if they did not already do so at Imbolc. Some plot out magical gardens to grow the herbs, flowers and vegetables that they will later harvest for feasting, ritual, and spellwork. As the first green shoots poke up through the soil, we truly begin the active half of the Wheel of the Year, turning our focus to outward action until the inward, passive half begins again at the Autumn Equinox.

Ostara is also a time to reflect on the balance between the male and female energies of the Universe, each of which requires the other to exist. This gender polarity is at the heart of traditional Wicca, with the Goddess and the God in constant cocreation throughout the changing of the seasons. At this point on the Wheel, the Goddess of the Earth is in her fertile Maiden aspect, while the Sun God grows into his maturity. There is a youthful joy between the two as they make their forays into romance and desire.

In some Wiccan traditions, this is the time when the divine pair comes together to conceive the next incarnation of the God, who will be born nine months later at Yule. In many others, the coupling of the divine pair happens at Beltane, when the new energies of growth and light have progressed further into wild abundance. Nonetheless, in Nature we see the mating of animals and insects is well underway as "spring fever" takes hold.

Fertility and the Goddess of the Dawn

As midpoints of the solar year, the equinoxes were not typically as widely celebrated as the solstices in pagan Europe. However, there are megalithic sites in many parts of the world that align with the Sun on this day.

Many ancient cultures in the Mediterranean region held festivals during this time, such as Sham el-Nessim, an Egyptian holiday that celebrates the beginning of Spring with origins dating back almost 5,000 years. In Persia, the festival of Nowruz (meaning

"new day") marked the Spring Equinox; it is still celebrated as the new year in Iran and in many other countries, and is a holy day for some faiths. The Jewish calendar sets the dates for Passover on a full-moon day—the fifteenth day of the Hebrew month of Nisan, which falls in March or April, and is the first month of the Hebrew lunisolar calendar.

In northern Europe, the Latvian festival of Lieldienas was a pre-Christian equinox holiday before it was absorbed into the Christian Easter. The Norse pagans are said to have honored their female deities with a festival called Dísablót, though some sources place this holiday at the Autumn Equinox or closer to Imbolc.

The Scandinavian tribes and the Anglo-Saxons are where most of our modern Ostara traditions come from, most particularly in the name of this Sabbat. An eighth-century scholar described a Saxon goddess named Eostre (also spelled Eostra) and mentions a feast held in her honor at springtime. Little is known about her, and even less is known about her Germanic equivalent, Ostara, for whom the month of April was named in ancient Germanic languages.

However, many place names in some Scandinavian countries suggest that this goddess was widely worshipped before the Christianization of Europe. The name Eostre has been translated as "east," "dawn," and "morning light," so she may have been a fitting deity to honor at the beginning of the growing season, even if much of the symbolism and lore about her in modern Wicca and other forms of Paganism has essentially been borrowed from better-known goddesses like the Norse Freya.

Symbols and customs of Ostara are recognizable to many as being part of the "Easter" season, such as the rabbit or hare and the egg—both symbols of fertility. The hare—a larger, more rural relative of the rabbit—is believed to be an ancient symbol of the Earth goddess archetype. Hares were also associated with the Moon, and in some places, witches were thought to be able to transform themselves into these quick-moving animals.

Hares and rabbits are associated with fertility because they are known for their fast and prolific reproductive abilities, but hare symbolism also has an element of honoring the Sun, as these usually nocturnal animals come out into the daylight during Spring to find their mates. Rabbits and eggs have traditionally been connected with each other both in ancient days and in modern Easter customs. This stems from our pagan ancestors' observations that plover eggs could sometimes be found in abandoned hares' "nests" in the wild.

The egg was a potent symbol of new beginnings and the promise of coming manifestations in many cultures. Creation myths in northern Europe, South Asia, West Africa, and the Middle East tell of the world being created from an egg. Deities were born from eggs in ancient Egyptian and Greek mythology. Painted eggs, representing fertility and new life, were part of the ancient Persian Nowruz celebrations. In Anglo-Saxon England, eggs were buried in gardens and under barns as a form of fertility and abundance magic. Offerings of eggs were made to female deities in ancient Scandinavia and in Germany.

Interestingly, the egg also speaks to the theme of balance at Ostara. It was once believed you could only stand eggs on their end at the Equinox, due to the gravitational forces of the Earth and the Sun at this time. Today, some still practice the tradition of standing an egg on its end in the moments right around the exact time of the Equinox.

Of all the Sabbats, Ostara is the clearest example of how the Christian churches appropriated pagan traditions in northern Europe in order to convert the population. By choosing Spring for its own celebration of renewal (in the form of Jesus's resurrection) and adopting the name of this older festival, it effectively absorbed this and other Spring Equinox holidays. However, as with Yule and Samhain, the old pagan customs and traditions have stubbornly stuck around and are even widely practiced in mainstream society.

Celebrating Ostara

As the weather grows warmer, Ostara is a particularly wonderful time to get outdoors and take in the seasonal changes taking place all around you. If you haven't been in the habit of noticing Spring's unfolding before, choose a place to visit regularly and study the transformation of the trees and other plant life. Greet the bees and other insects with joy as they begin to appear, and thank them for their role in sustaining life. Take every opportunity you can to watch the Sun set just a little later each evening. If you don't already have a garden to prepare, consider starting one—even if you only have a windowsill to grow a magical herb or two.

Coven rituals often focus on the goddess Ostara or another goddess of Spring. Witches may meet just before dawn to watch the Sun rise on this perfectly balanced day. Dyeing eggs is a fun activity to do with fellow Wiccans, perhaps using color correspondences to create magical eggs for later spellwork.

Natural objects are always a welcome part of rituals at any time of the year, but they are especially enjoyable at the Spring Equinox, the first Sabbat after Winter when flowers, buds, and blossoms are available for gathering. Sprinkle petals around your altar, let them float on water in your cauldron, and wear them in your hair if you like, but be careful to harvest Spring wildflowers responsibly, as they serve as much-needed food sources for our much-needed pollinators!

Ostara Correspondences

COLORS: Yellow, light green, light pink, blue, all pastel shades

STONES: Amethyst, aquamarine, jasper, moonstone, rose quartz

HERBS: Irish moss, lemongrass, meadowsweet, catnip, spearmint, cleavers, dogwood and ash trees, woodruff

FLOWERS: Daffodils, honeysuckle, iris, violets, Easter lilies, roses, dandelions, tulips, lilacs

INCENSE: Jasmine, rose, violet, lotus, magnolia, ginger, sage, strawberry, lemon

ALTAR DECORATIONS/SYMBOLS: Spring flowers, seeds, potted plants, colored eggs, rabbits/hares, birds, pinwheels, yellow discs, other solar symbols and imagery, ladybugs, bumblebees

FOODS: Eggs, honey, sprouts, dandelion greens, strawberries, all spring vegetables, pumpkin and sunflower seeds, pine nuts

BARK AND FLOWER BALANCING SPELL

Both the Spring and the Fall Equinoxes provide excellent opportunities to work for balance in our lives. This can mean achieving better physical health, learning how to deal more skillfully with an emotional challenge, or balancing the monthly budget.

Anything that is hindering your ability to make progress in the outer releasing so that the energies of positive manifestation have more room to come into your life. For best results, identify a goal that aligns with the physical, mental, or emotional realm to take full advantage of the magical correspondences of your chosen spring flower.

As for the bark, this should be gleaned (gathered from the ground) and *not* cut from a living tree. Many trees actively shed the bark at the onset of Spring to make room for their new growth. Trees associated with establishing balance include ash, birch, cedarwood, poplar, willow, and white oak. If none of these grow where you live, look up the magical correspondences of the trees that do grow in your area, or ask the God and Goddess to guide you in finding the right bark for this spell.

There are specific flowers and candle colors that are used for specific areas of life. For goals related to your mental well-being, use daffodil, iris, lilac, or violet with a yellow candle. For emotional matters, use crocus, daffodil, iris, violet, or tulip with a pink or light blue candle. For a goal related to the physical realm, use alpine aster, iris, honeysuckle, or lilac with a green candle.

=== YOU WILL NEED ===

Piece of gleaned tree bark

Pencil (or ink and quill)

Spell candle in a color corresponding to your goal

**Handful of petals from a flower
corresponding to your goal**

Start by meditating on your goal. What does *balance* in this situation or area of your life look and feel like to you? Identify a word or short phrase that encapsulates the achievement of your goal, such as "optimal health," "harmony in the home," or "all bills paid." Write this on the bark. Don't worry if the pencil doesn't show up, as you are still tracing the letters into the essence of the bark's energy.

Light the candle and lay the bark on your altar or work space. Sprinkle the flower petals around the bark in a circle three times, moving clockwise. With each rotation, say the following (or similar) words:

> *"As the day is balanced with the night,*
> *and the darkness balanced with the light,*
> *I find balance in my life."*

Allow the candle to burn out on its own, under supervision. Within 24 hours, return the bark to the Earth, either to where you found it or to another place in Nature.

OSTARA EGG GARDEN FERTILITY SPELL

Many cultures around the world have long traditions of using eggs in magic and for healing, divination, and protection, among other purposes. In this spell, you will combine the properties of fertility and new potential inherent to the egg with the growth-promoting energies that are so magnified at the height of Spring. For those already preparing their gardens, this is a highly opportune time to work this spell, as you're already out digging in the soil. If you don't have a garden, shift the focus to creating an abundant and thriving home, and bury the egg outside.

═ YOU WILL NEED ═

1 egg

Green marker or green paint and brush

═ INSTRUCTIONS ═

Hard-boil the egg, keeping in mind the specific intention for this spell. You might even say a blessing over the water before you start.

When the egg is dry and cool, draw a symbol of abundance appropriate to your goal—a flower or other plant, a house, a dollar sign or even the Sun—using the marker or paint. Once the symbol is dry, hold the egg in your hands and raise it toward the sky. Say the following (or similar) words:

> *"As the light and warmth increase,*
> *so does the bounty of my life.*
> *So let it be."*

Bury the egg in your garden or somewhere near the front door, visualizing golden light radiating from the egg throughout the soil, nourishing the roots of your growing plants or the foundation of your home.

≡ BELTANE ≡

NORTHERN HEMISPHERE DATES:
APRIL 30 OR MAY 1

SOUTHERN HEMISPHERE DATES:
OCT 31 OR NOV 1

PRONUNCIATION: *bee-YAWL-tinnuh* or *BELL-tinnuh*

THEMES: Passion, mischief, sensuality, sexuality, beauty, romance, fertility, vitality, abundance

ALSO KNOWN AS: May Day, Walpurgisnacht, Floralia, Calan Mai

By the time May 1 arrives in the Northern Hemisphere, Spring is in full swing, and the balance between the seasonal extremes is tipping toward Summer. The heat of the Sun increases with each day, and the Earth turns ever-deepening shades of green as buds and blossoms give way to the emerging new leaves. Flowers explode along the roadsides while birds, bees, and other flying creatures fill the air. And even if a stray chill sneaks back in for a day or two, there's still no going back—Winter is decidedly over.

In pre-modern times, May 1 marked the beginning of the light half of the year. For our Celtic ancestors, this day was the official start of Summer. Indeed, Beltane—or May Day as it is also known—is a time for exuberant celebration, as the long, warm days and the lush abundance of the growing season ramp up. The hopeful feeling that was kindled at Imbolc and built upon at Ostara now comes into full fruition.

Wiccans recognize Beltane as a time to celebrate the return of passion, vitality, fun, and frivolity as well as the cocreative energies of Nature that are so evident at this time of year. By this point, all living creatures have come out of hibernation and are enjoying the sunshine and the mild days. "Spring fever" is at its peak, as people find it hard to concentrate on their work or studies and long instead to spend all of their time outdoors. Primal urges toward lust and wildness become stronger, and we see both animals and humans pairing off, sparked by that most basic of instincts: to reproduce.

This life-giving relationship between masculine and feminine energies is honored now, perhaps more directly at this Sabbat than at any other point on the Wheel of the Year. In the cyclical story of the Goddess and the God, the shift from their mother–child relationship to that of partners in cocreation occurs. Over the Spring months, the God has matured into his young manhood, and the Goddess is again ready to step from her Maiden aspect into the life-giving Mother. In their prime of life, they fall in love and unite, and the Goddess once again becomes pregnant, ensuring the rebirth of the God after the current growing season comes to an end in the Autumn.

This is the act that brings about new life in the form of abundant crops, healthy livestock, and forests full of wild game and healing herbs. It is the fundamental building block of the continuation of life, and so is celebrated joyfully at this time by Wiccans and other Pagans alike. In some traditions, the union between the Goddess and God is seen as a divine marriage, and so handfastings—or Wiccan weddings—are customary at this time.

In addition to the Sun God and the Horned God (see page 103), many Wiccans and other pagans recognize an aspect of the God in the Green Man, an archetypal image of a male face camouflaged by leafy foliage. This mysterious face is found carved into very old buildings throughout Europe, including cathedrals, and is often connected with the Celtic god Cernunnos; however, variations of the image have been discovered all over the world. In early May, as leaves begin to emerge from the trees and shrubs, the return of the Green Man is imminent.

Soon the summer foliage will hide all that was visible during the bare months of Winter, and this greenery reminds us of the divinity hidden within plain sight. Perhaps for this reason, Beltane is also a time of the faeries, who are considered to be more active on this day than any other except for Samhain, which sits directly opposite the Wheel from Beltane. Faerie traditions can be traced back to the Irish *aos sí*, a name often translated as "faeries" or "spirits," but are found in various forms throughout ancient pagan cultures. They are said to inhabit various places in Nature, from hills and forests to small plants and flowers. Wiccans who are sensitive to the presence of faeries will leave offerings for them on Beltane Eve.

The Lighting of the Balefire

The name Beltane has been traced back to an old Celtic word meaning "bright fire." Some scholars believe it to be related to the ancient Sun god Belenus, whose name has been translated as "bright shining one." Belenus was worshipped throughout Celtic Europe, and his feast day was on May 1, so this connection seems logical, though not all historians accept it. For one thing, Belenus (also known as Bel or Beil) doesn't make significant appearances in the mythology of the areas where Beltane was historically celebrated: Ireland, Scotland, and the Isle of Man. He was much more significant to the Gaulish Celts of the European continent, where the festivals celebrated on May 1 are known by different names.

Nonetheless, the ritual importance of fire was a central focus of Beltane for the ancient Celts of the westernmost islands, where the first references to the holiday are found. The chief event at Beltane in ancient Ireland was the lighting of the balefire on the eve of May 1, the first fire of the light half of the Celtic year. To prepare for this event, every household hearth was extinguished. In one legend, tribal representatives from all over Ireland met at the hill of Uisneach, a sacred site where a giant bonfire was lit. Each representative would light a torch from the great fire and carry it back to their village, where the people waited in the darkness. From the village torch, each household would then relight their home fires so that all of Ireland was set alight from the same flame. In another version of this story, the fire at Uisneach could be seen from several miles away in every direction, signaling to the surrounding villages to light their own central fires, which was then spread throughout their communities. Both traditions marked the beginning of Summer, with hopes for plentiful sunshine throughout the season.

As a living symbol of the Sun, ritual fire was considered to have magical powers. In many Celtic areas, the Beltane fires were used for ritual purification of cattle before they were turned out into the summer pastures. The cattle were driven between two large bonfires, which were tended by Druids who used special incantations to imbue the fires with sacred energy. The fire would clear the animals of any lingering winter disease and protect them from illness and accidents throughout the Summer. People would also walk between the fires, or jump over them, for luck and fertility

through the coming year. In some areas, the ashes from the smoldering fire would be sprinkled over crops, livestock, and the people themselves.

Over time, the annual lighting of the Beltane fires grew into larger festivals, where people came to greet each other after the long Winter. Dancing, music, games, and great feasts became traditions, along with a free license for sexual promiscuity on this special occasion. Other customs observed at this time included eating "Beltane bannock," a special oatcake that bestowed an abundant growing season and protection of livestock, and making a "May Bush," a branch or bough from a tree decorated with brightly colored ribbons, flowers, and eggshells. People would dance around the May Bush on Beltan, and then either place it by the front door for luck or burn it in the bonfire. This is believed to be a remnant of Druidic tradition, which held many trees to be sacred and to possess magical qualities. A related custom involved hanging a rowan branch over the hearth or weaving it into the ceiling to protect the house for the coming year.

In general, trees, herbs, and flowers played a part at Beltane and at other May Day celebrations throughout Europe. People gathered primrose flowers and hawthorne and hazel blossoms, placed them at doors and windows, made them into garlands, and even used them to adorn cattle. Yellow flowers were prized for their association with the Sun.

Herbs gathered on this day were said to be especially potent for magic and healing, especially if picked at dawn or while the morning dew was still on them. The "May dew" inspired a variety of traditions around beauty. Young women would roll naked in the dew or collect it to wash their faces with, as it was said to purify the skin, maintain youthful looks, and help attract a romantic partner.

Celebrating Beltane

Today's Beltane celebrations draw from various traditions across the pagan landscape of Europe. While bonfires remain a big part of most rituals, Wiccan and other Pagan observances don't necessarily borrow as heavily from Celtic lore at Beltane as they do at Imbolc or Samhain.

Typically, public celebrations incorporate traditions from Germanic cultures—especially dancing around the Maypole, a very tall, circular pole made, ideally, from wood. The Maypole features in many May Day festivities, both Pagan and secular alike. At the top of the pole hang ribbons of various colors, and each participant holds one ribbon as they circle the pole in an interweaving dance, until they have decorated its length with ribbons.

This practice is rooted in customs found in England, where the cross-quarter day is known as May Day. The Maypole would be erected in the center of the village or in a nearby field and decorated with flowers and branches brought in from the fields, gardens, and forests. The villagers rose at dawn to gather these symbols of Summer and used them to decorate their homes and their bodies as well. Women braided flowers into their hair, and both men and women—especially those who were young and unmarried—put extra effort into grooming themselves for the big day. It was traditionally young people who did the dancing around the Maypole, and any woman who wanted to conceive a child was sure to be among them. In the earliest times, the dancing would have been a looser, simpler affair. The more intricately involved dance with the entwining ribbons came about only in the nineteenth century.

Wiccans and other Pagans recognize the pole itself as a supremely phallic symbol, representing the God at the height of

his powers. The garlands and greenery symbolize the Goddess and her fertility. As the dancers come together, the ribbons gradually encircle the pole until it is symbolically wrapped in the womb of the Earth. In this way, the whole community enacts the union between the divine pair.

However, this association with phallic symbolism is a somewhat recent development. Historians believe that the Maypole originated with fertility rituals of ancient Germanic tribes, who would at one time have been dancing around a young living tree as opposed to a cut pole. The tradition evolved over the centuries after being brought to England, when in the seventeenth century a mistaken association was made between the Maypole and the bawdier customs of ancient Rome. The phallic symbolism has been part of the lore of May Day ever since, especially among Witches.

Covens have bonfires when possible, often lighting a candle first to represent the "old fire" of the past seasons. The candle is extinguished, and the bonfire ushers in the "new fire"—the new energies of the coming year. These energies are typically masculine, but there is also an emphasis on the cauldron as a symbol of the Goddess. A cauldron may be present at the bonfire, perhaps holding water, herbs, or flowers. Alternatively, a small fire may be lit within the cauldron itself.

The gender polarity of Wicca is especially evident at Beltane, and the sexual union of the God and Goddess is symbolically enacted by the joining of the athame with the chalice. Literal coupling—or the Great Rite—is also practiced, though not as commonly. As Wicca becomes more expansive, some traditions are less focused on gender polarity to accommodate the perspectives of gay, transgender, and nonbinary people.

The rich lore surrounding Beltane offers an abundance of ways to celebrate this Sabbat. A fire is appropriate, whether it's an outdoor bonfire, a small fire in a cauldron or heat-resistant bowl, or

a host of lit candles. Decorate your altar and your home with green branches and flowers gathered in the early morning, and fill a cauldron or large bowl with water and float fresh blossom petals on top.

It's a good time for beauty rituals, so concoct a facial scrub or mask with dried herbs and fresh water from a stream or spring, or braid your hair to represent the coming together of the Goddess and the God. Make an offering of nuts, berries and fruit for the faeries and leave it under a tree in your yard or in the woods. Tie colored ribbons to young tree branches to make wishes for the coming season. Spend some time with your lover outdoors or work magic to bring a lover into your life. Above all, enjoy the warmth in the air and the accelerating growth of the natural world!

Beltane Correspondences

COLORS: Light and deep greens, yellow, light blue, red and white for the God and Goddess

STONES: Malachite, amber, orange carnelian, sapphire, rose quartz

HERBS: Birch trees, hawthorn, honeysuckle, rosemary

FLOWERS: Yellow cowslip, lily of the valley, lilac, hyacinth, daisies, roses

INCENSE: Lilac, frankincense, jasmine, african violet, sage, mugwort

ALTAR DECORATIONS/SYMBOLS: Maypole, ribbons, garlands, spring flowers, young plants, Goddess and God statues

FOODS: Oatmeal cakes, bannock and other bread, dairy, strawberries, cherries, spring greens

BELTANE ABUNDANCE DIVINATION

The core theme of Beltane is the fruitful abundance created by the union of the Goddess and the God. You can ask these divine energies for wisdom in helping you manifest personal abundance during the coming season. This divination also gives you a great opportunity to talk to them using your own words, which will help you deepen your personal relationship with them. You can use different colors for the deity candles, such as orange and green, if they resonate more with you.

═ YOU WILL NEED ═

1 work candle for atmosphere (optional)

Small heatproof plate

1 red candle (to represent the God)

1 white candle (to represent the Goddess)

Light the work candle, if using. Place the plate between the two deity candles. Light the Goddess candle, speaking words of greeting to her as you do so. (You can look up some invocations or simply freestyle it.) Light the God candle and greet him in a similar manner. Spend some time talking to your deities about your hopes for the coming season. Ask any questions you have about abundance-related issues or developments in your life.

When the candles have accumulated enough melted wax, pick them up together and gently tilt them over the plate, pouring in overlapping circles so that the colors mingle together. You may want to do this a few times as the candles continue to burn lower. When the wax has dried, look carefully for images and symbols that can point you in the direction of your stated goals. You can allow the candles to burn out on their own, or gently extinguish them and use them for atmospheric lighting in future rituals or spellwork.

HERBAL CHARM FOR FINDING ROMANCE

Beltane is a great time to work magic for new love. This charm is for single people who don't currently have a love prospect in mind. Be careful not to misuse it as a "snare" for someone you have your eye on, or it will backfire!

If you're handy with a needle and thread, you can add power to the charm by sewing a sachet in the shape of a heart, but the drawstring bag will work just fine.

1 teaspoon dried lavender buds
1 teaspoon dried hibiscus flowers
1 teaspoon dried damiana leaves
1 cinnamon stick
Small drawstring bag, ideally red or pink
Small piece of rose quartz and/or garnet

≡ INSTRUCTIONS ≡

Pour the herbs into a small cauldron or bowl. Mix them together with your fingertips to work your personal energy into the herbs. Stir three times, clockwise, with the cinnamon stick. Then pour the herb mixture into the bag and add the stones. As you close the bag, say the following (or similar) words:

> *"Herb and stone,*
> *flesh and bone,*
> *bring new love*
> *into my home."*

Keep the charm in your bedroom and bring it with you when you go out in public until you meet your next romantic partner. If you like, grate the cinnamon stick over food or a beverage to add some romantic energy to it, or use it as a stirring tool for other spellwork.

═ LITHA ═

SUMMER SOLSTICE

NORTHERN HEMISPHERE:
JUNE 20-22

SOUTHERN HEMISPHERE:
DECEMBER 20-23

PRONUNCIATION: *LEE-tha*

THEMES: Abundance, growth, masculine energy, love, magic

ALSO KNOWN AS: Midsummer, Midsummer's Eve, Gathering Day, St. John's Day, St. John's Eve, Summer Solstice, Alban Hefin, Feill-Sheathain

Litha, also known in the wider Pagan world as Midsummer, is celebrated on the day of the Summer Solstice—the longest day and shortest night of the solar year.

This is the height of Summer, when the days are warm and plentiful. Abundance can be found everywhere—the crops are in full growth as we get closer to the beginning of the harvest season, and the fields and forests are bursting with animal and plant life. The Sun reaches its highest point, which means the days will now begin to grow shorter again until we reach the Winter Solstice at Yule. But there's no need to think about Winter just now—instead, we celebrate our place on this warm and lively side of the Wheel.

This is the time of the God's greatest power, whether we focus on the light and heat of his Sun God aspect; his role as the Green

Man, lush with thick foliage; or the Horned God, strong and agile at the heart of the forest. There is a potent masculine energy to be tapped here, if we wish.

At the same time, the Goddess is in her Mother aspect, as the generous Earth yields abundant blessings of food, flowers, and striking natural beauty. We feel the love of this divine pair easily and often in these easy, breezy days of Midsummer.

Magical and medicinal herbs are said to be at the height of their power and are traditionally gathered on this day to be dried and stored for use in the Winter. Many people also feel the energies of the faeries at this time—a slightly mischievous "something" in the air that Shakespeare once captured in *A Midsummer Night's Dream*.

The Power of the Sun

Many Pagan sources regarding Litha assert that the Celts celebrated Midsummer in much the same way that they observed their four cross-quarter festivals, but there isn't much evidence to support this idea. Nonetheless, the number of Neolithic stone monuments found throughout Europe that align with the Sun on this day—in both Celtic and non-Celtic lands—indicates that the Summer Solstice was significant to our ancient ancestors.

The most well-known example is Stonehenge in England, where from the center of the circle, the Midsummer Sun can be seen rising over the giant Heel Stone. Today, Pagans of many different traditions gather at Stonehenge on the eve of the Summer Solstice, celebrating throughout the night as they await the sunrise. However, it's unlikely that any of the rituals taking place in modern times are connected to the actual history of Stonehenge.

When it comes to the activities of the ancient Germanic tribes, however, much more is known. The solstice would have

been great cause for celebration, especially in the northernmost regions of Europe, as the near-endless daylight of the height of Summer made for such contrast with the long, dark winters. In a world without electricity and artificial lighting, the Sun's light would have been unimaginably precious. We can see this in the fire-centered traditions that have come down from Norse, Anglo-Saxon, and other Germanic peoples and are still practiced today. Many of these have inspired the Litha celebrations of Wiccans and other modern Pagans.

Aside from the Sun, and to a lesser extent the Moon, fire was the only source of light available to people until the nineteenth century. Fire is the symbolic manifestation of the Sun on Earth. It is both tangible and untouchable, miraculous yet dangerous, and it demands respect. Our pagan ancestors—the Norse in particular—honored the Element of Fire at Midsummer with bonfires and torchlight processions, parading with their families, communities, and even animals to their ritual sites for the evening's celebrations. The fires were believed to keep away evil spirits and misfortune. In Anglo-Saxon tradition, boys would roam the fields with their torches to drive away dragons who threatened their springs and wells.

A long-standing tradition in many parts of Europe was the "sunwheel," a giant wagon wheel, tar barrel, or ball of straw that was set alight and rolled down a steep hill into a river or other body of water. The significance of this ritual has several possible interpretations. Some suggest it symbolized the annual journey of the Sun—after reaching the zenith of the solstice, it now makes its way back down toward its lowest point at Yule. Others believe it encouraged a natural balance between the Elements of Fire and Water, acknowledging the need for rain to nourish the crops and prevent drought.

The Solstice is still observed today throughout northern Europe with a variety of rituals dating back to pre-Christian times. Bonfires are held on beaches or near waterways in Denmark and Finland, while in Poland, young girls throw wreaths of flowers into lakes, rivers, and the Baltic Sea. In many of these countries, the celebrations begin in the evening and last throughout the night until the Sun rises the following morning. In many places, the day is known as St. John's Day, after the Christian feast established in the fourth century CE, but the pagan roots of the holiday are still clearly recognizable in today's festivities.

The name Litha is a modern innovation, borrowed by Wiccans from an old Saxon word for this time of year. Many Wiccans and other Pagans use the more traditional *Midsummer*, as this date falls in the middle of the Summer, even though our modern calendars designate this as the start of the season.

Celebrating Litha

If there's one thing you should put on your Litha to-do list, it's to get outdoors and enjoy the summer weather. Even if your actual ritual must be held inside, you can prepare yourself energetically by attuning with the Sun's light ahead of time. It's ideal to spend some time by a river or other body of water, especially if it's a sunny day. Watch the sunrise and the sunset if you can. Many people like to stay up the whole night before in order to see the Sun rise on its most powerful day.

If the weather won't be fair on the solstice day, you can commune with Nature the day before or after. But if you're experiencing a string of rainy days, don't fret—the Sun is always there behind the clouds, and you can acknowledge that specifically in your ritual, if you wish.

Covens located near a coastline may meet at the shore for their Litha celebrations, in honor of the balance between the Elements of Fire and Water. Rituals are ideally held outdoors, and groups may meet at sunrise on this day, or at "solar noon," the point in the day when the Sun is at its highest in the sky.

One common ritual acts out the story of the battle between the Oak King and the Holly King. In some Wiccan traditions, these twin aspects of the Sun God's annual journey take turns ruling the year. The Oak King, representing the light half of the year, reigns until the Summer Solstice, when he is cut down by the Holly King, who heralds the beginning of the waning of the light. The ritual enactment serves as a reminder that there can be no light without the dark—it is the contrast between the two that makes each possible.

Magic is, of course, always an appropriate part of Sabbat celebrations, but at Litha the energies available from the abundant natural world are particularly potent. Plug into these currents with spellwork of your choosing. You may want to focus on goals related to love, beauty, friendship, healing, empowerment, or physical and magical energy, but all purposes are suitable at this time.

If you work with the faeries, be sure to acknowledge their presence with offerings of food and drink. The height of Summer is a great time to watch the subtle movements of the trees in the wind. You just may see a faerie face or two—or even the Green Man himself—among the leaves. If you grow your own herbs or know how to recognize them in the wild, make a point of gathering a few on this day to use in magical teas, charms, and other workings.

Making protective amulets is a popular magical tradition at this time. Wiccans and other Pagans tie a trio of protective herbs together with cloth to carry or wear around the neck for the coming year. The amulet is charged over the Midsummer bonfire (or a candle, if need be). After the year is up, it is buried before a new one is made. You can make another type of amulet with the ashes of the Litha fire by carrying them in a pouch or kneading them into soft clay that is then baked in a kiln. Litha ashes also make great fertilizer for your garden.

Be sure to incorporate the Element of Fire into your magic, whether with a large ritual bonfire or a few simple candles. If it's a cloudy day, light a candle first thing in the morning and leave it to burn until sunset. This is a good time for clearing and charging crystals and other magical tools by leaving them in sunlight for a few hours. Divination related to love and romance is also traditional at this time, as are rituals of rededication to the God and Goddess.

Litha Correspondences

COLORS: Gold, green, red, orange, yellow, blue

STONES: Emerald, amber, tiger's eye, jade

HERBS: St. John's wort, mugwort, vervain, mint, thyme, chamomile, parsley, oak and holly trees, lavender

FLOWERS: All flowers, but especially rose, honeysuckle, daisy, lily

INCENSE: Pine, myrrh, rose, cedar, frankincense, lemon, sage, lavender

ALTAR DECORATIONS/SYMBOLS: Roses, sunflowers, berries, oak and holly leaves, birds, butterflies, seashells, pinwheels, yellow discs, other solar symbols and imagery

FOODS: Early summer fruits and vegetables, honey cakes, strawberries, fennel, lemon balm tea, red wine

SUMMER SOLSTICE COURAGE SPELL

With its long days of light and warmth, Summer is a time for action and outwardly focused energy. This is the perfect time of year to take on a project, enterprise, or issue that you've been putting off due to fear of failure or fear of change. Whether you want to ask for a raise, learn to play a new instrument, go back to school, or get to the bottom of a problematic relationship, the energy of the Sun can help you tap into and strengthen your innate courage to dive into the task at hand.

At one point or another, everyone has some fear—whether conscious or unconscious—holding them back from achieving certain goals in life. The fiery essence of the Sun is both purifying and fortifying, allowing you to release your fears and strengthen your sense of well-being regardless of your circumstances. This is the optimal state of mind from which to approach any kind of challenge, such as solving a problem or enriching your life with a new activity. The Sun card in the Tarot represents power, practicality, freedom, and well-being. If you have a Tarot deck, pull out the Sun card and focus on its imagery in preparation for the spellwork.

This spell is suitable any time during the height of Summer, but it is extra powerful if you work it on the day of the Solstice. For spectacular magic, gather your herbs on this day as well, whether you grow them in your garden or purchase them at the market. (You can also see if any of them grow near you in the wild.) Dried herbs will work fine, but in the spirit of lush summer abundance, strive for fresh if possible. It's ideal to use all four of these herbs, which are associated both with courage and with the magical energies of this Sabbat, but if this isn't possible, try to incorporate at least three.

1 white work candle
Sun Tarot card (optional)
1 teaspoon chopped fresh lavender
1 teaspoon chopped fresh vervain
1 teaspoon chopped fresh St. John's wort
1 teaspoon chopped fresh thyme
Small bowl for mixing herbs
1 orange spell or votive candle
Small heatproof plate

=== INSTRUCTIONS ===

Light the work candle. Prop up the Sun card (if using) where you can see it while you work the spell.

Spend a few moments thinking about what it is you want to achieve and how you will feel when you've succeeded. Hold this feeling in mind as you add the herbs to the bowl, one at a time, mixing them together with your fingertips.

Now hold the orange candle in both hands and charge it with your personal energy. Visualize yourself outside in full sunlight, basking in the warmth and infused with bright light throughout your entire being. Send this light into the candle. When you feel ready, place the candle (in a secure holder) on the plate.

Starting at the northernmost point, sprinkle the herbs in a clockwise circle around the base of the candle as you say the following (or similar) words:

"As the Sun shines bright at the height of its power,
so my courage comes forth to light the way."

Now, state your goal out loud as if you've already achieved it. (For example, "I have enrolled in college classes to advance my career" or "I have embarked on a healthier eating plan.") Then light the candle and say, "So it is."

Leave the candle to burn out on its own, under supervision. You can sprinkle the herbs onto the Earth or burn them in your cauldron.

LITHA ANOINTING OIL

This magical oil can be made at Litha and used year round to harness the powerful energies of the height of Summer. Use natural essential oils rather than synthetic fragrance oils, if at all possible.

It's wise to do a patch test with your oil blend first to make sure it won't irritate your skin, especially if you have sensitive skin. Dab a cotton swab in the oil blend and apply it to your inner wrist or behind your knee. Place a waterproof adhesive bandage over the spot and leave in place for 24 hours. (If any irritation occurs, remove the bandage and wash the area with soap and water, and refrain from using the oil again.) **Note that citrus oils (such as lemon, bergamot, and orange) are photosensitive, meaning they can burn your skin when exposed to sunlight. It's best to stick to nighttime magic when using citrus oils, and avoid use if the citrus oil or a blend containing a citrus oil is exposed to sunlight. Also note: Avoid using lavender oil during the first trimester of pregnancy.**

2 tablespoons sunflower oil
Clean glass container
4 drops lavender essential oil
3 drops lemon essential oil
1 drop rose essential oil
Small funnel
Brown glass bottle

≡ INSTRUCTIONS ≡

Pour the sunflower oil into a clean glass jar. Then add one essential oil at a time, taking a moment to inhale the aroma as you swirl the oils together in the jar, building an increasingly complex scent as you go.

Funnel your newly created blend into a brown glass bottle, seal tightly, and let it sit outside in the shade for one hour. If you clear and charge your crystals under the Litha Sun, try anointing them with the oil blend afterward and use the anointed crystals in charms and other spellwork.

≡ LAMMAS ≡

PRONUNCIATION: *LAH-mahs*

THEMES: First fruits, harvest, gratitude, benevolent sacrifice, utilizing skills and talents

ALSO KNOWN AS: Lughnasa (or Lughnasadh), August Eve, Feast of Bread, Harvest Home, Gŵyl Awst, First Harvest

Situated on the opposite side of the Wheel from Imbolc, which heralds the end of the Winter season, Lammas marks the beginning of Summer's end. It is the cross-quarter day between the Summer Solstice and the Autumn Equinox.

Although the days are still hot, sunshine is still abundant, and the fields and forests are still teeming with life, we can begin to feel the telltale signs of the approaching Autumn. The Sun sets earlier with each passing day, and many plants begin to wither, dropping their seeds to the ground so that new life can return at the start of the next growing season. Berries, apples, and other fruits begin to ripen on trees and vines, and the grain in the fields has reached its full height, ready to be cut down and stored for the Winter. This is a bittersweet time, as we are surrounded by the abundance of the Summer's bounty, yet becoming more aware by the day that we are heading back into the dark time of year.

Lammas is the time of the "first fruits" and is known in Wiccan and other Pagan traditions as the first of the three harvest festivals. Grain crops will soon be ready for harvesting, if they aren't already, along with corn and many other late-summer vegetables and early-Autumn fruits. Of course, plenty of produce has already been available for harvesting, and plenty more will be ready later on in the season. But Lammas marks the point in time when

harvesting, rather than planting or tending, becomes the main focus.

This is a time to consciously recognize the fruits of our labors—whether literally or metaphorically—and to give thanks for all that has manifested. We recognize the inherent sacrifice of the plants that give their lives so that we may eat, and we are humbled by the greater life-and-death cycles that govern all of creation.

Just six weeks after the Summer Solstice, the God at Lammas is now visibly on the wane. He is approaching his old age, rising later each morning and retiring sooner every night. The Goddess in her Mother aspect is still waxing, as the Earth continues to bear the fruit of the seeds planted at the start of the growing season. She is still pregnant with the new God, who will be born at Yule, after the old God completes his journey to the Underworld at Samhain. This is one of the most poignant moments on the Wheel of the Year, as the Goddess demonstrates that life goes on even though we all experience loss and the fading of the light.

In ancient agricultural civilizations, grain was often associated with the death and rebirth cycle, and many Wiccan mythological traditions draw on this archetype at Lammas. In one version, the Sun God transfers his power to the living grain in the fields, and so is sacrificed when the grain is cut down. The God willingly sacrifices himself so that his people may live.

And yet the God is later reborn, ensuring that the crops will grow once again to feed the people for another year. The harvest practice of saving seed grain for planting next year's crop is both a practical necessity and a way of participating in the metaphor—saving the seeds is a way of ensuring the God's rebirth.

The First Fruits

In the modern world, the first of August is not necessarily an important harvest date and may seem quite early to some. After all, Summer is still in full swing, and due to our advanced agricultural technology, there are now multiple growing cycles for various types of grain and other crops.

But back when harvesting, threshing, winnowing, and sieving of the grain was all done by hand, farmers needed to start as early as they could. Once this hard work was done, it would be time to bring in the later-season crops ahead of the first killing frosts. August 1 wasn't necessarily a hard and fast date for our ancestors to start this work, though it was considered the earliest acceptable time to begin bringing in the wheat. If the crop wasn't quite ready, due to insufficient rain or sunshine, then the harvest—and the accompanying festivities—would wait. Nature's schedule was far more powerful than any calendar humans could devise.

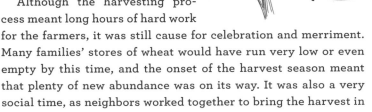

Although the harvesting process meant long hours of hard work for the farmers, it was still cause for celebration and merriment. Many families' stores of wheat would have run very low or even empty by this time, and the onset of the harvest season meant that plenty of new abundance was on its way. It was also a very social time, as neighbors worked together to bring the harvest in successfully for everyone in the community. Feasting was a must, and a special emphasis was placed on bread as a staple of nourishment that would provide for the family throughout the long Winter months and beyond.

The first loaves made from the first wheat of the new season were particularly significant, and in Anglo-Saxon England, these loaves were brought into churches and laid on the altar to be blessed. This is where the holiday gets its name—the old Saxon phrase *hlaf-maesse*, which translates literally to "loaf mass" and eventually became "Lammas." The custom of blessing the bread makes Lammas an interesting example of how Christianity and pagan religions coexisted for a time.

Bread is an important symbol in many spiritual traditions, going back to the ancient world. For Wiccans and other modern Pagans, bread is representative of all the Elements: the seeds growing in the Earth, the yeast using Water and Air to make the dough rise, and the Fire of the hearth making the finished product. Add to this the concept of Akasha—or Spirit—being present in the grain thanks to the power of the Sun, and you have a very sacred food indeed. Bread is also significant in Christian communion rituals of the Christian churches, but if Christian officials had hoped to replace pagan practices with the "loaf mass," they didn't succeed, at least not immediately. The Anglo-Saxon peasants were known to use their church-blessed bread in protection rituals and other magic.

As an agricultural festival, the First Harvest would certainly have preceded the arrival of Christianity to Europe, yet it's unknown what this holiday was called in England prior to the custom that brought about its name. However, in Ireland, the day was, and still is, known as Lughnasa (pronounced *LOO-na-sa* or *Loo-NOSS-ah*). This cross-quarter festival was held as a tribute

to the Celtic God Lugh, a warrior deity who was associated with the Sun, fire, grain, and many skills and talents such as smithcraft, building, music, and magic. The association with grain comes from Lugh's foster mother, Tailtiu, who was said to have cleared the plains of Ireland for use in agriculture and died of exhaustion from doing so.

Lugh held an annual harvest festival in her honor, which included athletic games and contests that resembled the original Olympics, along with music and storytelling. The ancient Celts made this mythical festival real, and it was celebrated in one form or another well into the twentieth century.

As with other ancient harvest festivals, Lughnasa was a time to offer the "first fruits" to the gods. The first of the crops were carried to the top of a high hill and buried there. Communities gathered bilberries and sacrificed a sacred bull for the great feast. They performed ritual plays in which Lugh defeated blight or famine and seized the harvest for the people. Dancing, drinking, trading, and matchmaking were popular activities at the gatherings, which might last for three days before coming to a close. Handfastings and trial marriages (which lasted a year and a day and could then be broken or made permanent) were also common, as were visits to holy wells, where people prayed for good health and left offerings of coins or cloth strips.

Celebrating Lammas

Across the spectrum of Wiccan and other modern Pagan traditions, celebrations at Lammas can vary widely. Those inspired by the ancient Celts may choose to focus on honoring Lugh, and many call this holiday Lughnasa rather than Lammas. Others might be more rooted in Anglo-Saxon traditions, while still others incorporate a blend of ancient sources into their practice. Among all this diversity, however, the central theme is almost always the first harvest and the transition into the darker, colder months.

Feasts are part of every Sabbat, but they are particularly important during the harvest holidays, as we give thanks to the God and Goddess for the bounty of the Earth. Wiccans deliberately choose to prepare and savor the first "fruits" of the harvest season, whether they be apples and grapes, wheat and corn, or anything else that has come into season where they live. This feast is a physical participation in the turning of the Wheel of the Year, as we recognize that this time of newly reaped abundance, like all other moments in time, will soon pass.

Coven rituals at Lammas often honor the waxing energy of the pregnant Goddess and the waning energy of the fading God. They give thanks for the manifestations of the year thus far, whether material, spiritual, or both. In some traditions, practitioners state goals for the next two harvest Sabbats and intentions for the bounty of the Earth to be shared by all beings. For solitary practitioners, a full-scale feast may be somewhat impractical, especially for those who live alone. If this is the case, you can still make a point of enjoying some fresh baked bread and late-summer fruits and vegetables as part of your Lammas celebration. Save any seeds from the fruits for planting, or use them in your spellwork.

Another way to mark this Sabbat is to make a corn dolly from corn stalks or straw. This is a manifestation of the ancient "Corn Mother" archetype found around the world. She can be placed on your altar and even used in magic. Since crafting is a way of honoring the Celtic god Lugh at this time, consider making or decorating other ritual items, such as a wand or pentacle. You could also choose to practice any of your skills and talents, whether that means writing, playing an instrument, playing in a soccer or basketball game, or simply going for a nice long run. If there's a new skill you'd like to learn, now is a great time to get started.

Whatever you do, be sure to spend some time outdoors drinking in the sights, sounds, and smells of Summer because they will fade away before you know it!

Lammas Correspondences

COLORS: Gold, yellow, orange, red, green, light brown

STONES: Carnelian, citrine, peridot, aventurine, sardonyx

HERBS: Sage, meadowsweet, ginseng, vervain, calendula, fenugreek, heather, dill, yarrow

FLOWERS: Sunflower, passionflower, acacia flowers, cyclamen

INCENSE: Sandalwood, frankincense, copal, rose, rose hips, rosemary, chamomile, passionflower

ALTAR DECORATIONS/SYMBOLS: First harvest fruits and vegetables, fresh baked bread, grapes and vines, corn dollies, sickles and scythes, Lugh's spear, symbols representing your own skills

FOODS: Apples, breads, all grains, berries, hazelnuts, summer squash, corn, elderberry wine, ale

LAMMAS GRATITUDE AND BREAD BLESSING RITUAL

As anyone who practices gratitude on a regular basis will tell you, it pays to express appreciation for the blessings in your life. This is because of the Law of Attraction—the more you appreciate, the more you attract new things and circumstances to appreciate! It's also good to express gratitude simply for its own sake. Any Sabbat is an excellent occasion to do so, but it's especially appropriate at Lammas, the season of the first fruits. This ritual provides a simple, elegant structure for thanking the God and Goddess, Nature, or whatever your term may be for the powers that govern the Universe. If seven candles are too many to manage, you can certainly use fewer, but it's nice to get a little decadent if you can.

≡ YOU WILL NEED ≡

7 gold, yellow, and orange candles (any size and in any combination of these three colors)

Handful of fresh sunflower and/or calendula petals

Loaf of fresh-baked bread

Pen (or pencil) and writing paper

Arrange the candles and sprinkle the petals among them in a manner that pleases you. Place the bread in front of the candles and light one of them.

Now, make a list of at least ten blessings you've experienced over the past few months. These can be hugely significant or "little" things. Usually, your list will have a combination of both. You will likely find that more and more things occur to you as you write (again, the Law of Attraction at work). When you've got your list together, light the rest of the candles and then read the list aloud, starting with "Thank you for…" before each item.

Now, hold the bread up toward the sky and say the following (or similar) words:

"God and Goddess, I thank you for this bread,
which represents all the blessings I have listed here and more.
May all on Earth be nourished by the bounty of Nature.
So let it be."

Eat some of the bread and be sure to use the rest of it over the coming days.

SKILL-BUILDING CRYSTAL CHARM

In the spirit of Lugh, the god of many skills, this simple charm can support you in developing or strengthening any skill, whether it's related to work or leisure. You can use any crystal or mineral stone you feel an affinity with, but choosing one with Lammas associations makes for a nice extra boost at this time of year.

The correspondences for the crystals you can use in this charm include aventurine for confidence, creativity, and luck; citrine for joy and success; and sardonyx for strength and willpower.

Note that lemon oil is photosensitive, so avoid using lemon oil if your skin will be exposed to sunlight. (See page 78 for more information about conducting a patch test and photosensitive oils.)

≡ YOU WILL NEED ≡

Oil blend containing lemon, spearmint, eucalyptus, or other "activating" essential oil

1 small or medium-sized crystal

1 red or yellow candle

≡ INSTRUCTIONS ≡

Anoint the candle and the crystal with the oil. Hold the crystal in your dominant hand and feel its energies moving through you. Visualize yourself being highly proficient in your chosen skill. Hold this feeling in your heart as you light the candle. Place the crystal in front of the candle and allow the candle to burn out on its own. Keep your crystal with you whenever you're practicing your skill, and rub it with your thumb whenever you need a little boost of confidence.

☰ MABON ☰

FALL EQUINOX

NORTHERN HEMISPHERE:
SEPTEMBER 21-23

SOUTHERN HEMISPHERE:
MARCH 19-21

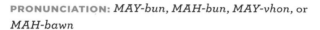

PRONUNCIATION: *MAY-bun, MAH-bun, MAY-vhon,* or *MAH-bawn*

THEMES: Harvest, gratitude, abundance, balance, preparation, welcoming the dark

ALSO KNOWN AS: Autumnal Equinox, Fall Equinox, September Equinox, Harvest Tide, Harvest Home, Harvest Festival, Wine Harvest, Feast of Avalon, Alben Elfed, Meán Fómhair, Gwyl canol Hydref

Wiccans and many other modern Pagans use the name Mabon for the Sabbat falling at the Autumn Equinox. Compared to the solstices, which occur during the middle of their respective seasons, the equinoxes mark more significant shifts from one season to the next.

By this point on the Wheel, the end of Summer has become undeniable—a crisp chill in the air descends each evening at sunset, and the leaves on deciduous trees have begun to turn deep, bright shades of red, yellow, and orange. The blue of the afternoon sky deepens as the Summer's white-hot sunlight turns golden. Plant life dies back in gardens, fields, and forests, and squirrels get busy gathering acorns and walnuts to stash away for the coming cold months.

For many people, this is a time of mixed emotions, as the beauty of the transforming Earth reminds us that we're heading back into the bleak and barren months. But this is the true essence of the seasons and the Wheel—all of creation is always in motion, and the only constant in life is change.

The cyclical nature of time is especially apparent at Mabon as we work with themes that echo Lammas and Ostara. Mabon is the second of the three harvest festivals, representing the pinnacle of abundance when it comes to the crops of the fields and the bounty of our gardens. Once again, we take time to appreciate all we have manifested—material and otherwise—through our efforts over the past several months.

There is more to do between now and Samhain to prepare for the Winter. This is a good time to take stock and evaluate what plans and projects need to be brought to completion before we enter the dark half of the year. It's also a moment to pause and celebrate what has taken place thus far. In doing so, we give thanks to those who have assisted us, whether they be friends, family, or spirit guides and ancestors on the other side. And we recognize the importance of sharing our good fortune with others, by hosting feasts as well as giving to those in need.

The other central focus at this time is balance. Like Ostara, which falls on the Spring Equinox, Mabon marks the point when day and night are of equal length. This time, the Sun crosses the "celestial equator" and appears to head south. From now until Yule, the light will wane significantly, with the nights becoming noticeably longer than the days.

Interestingly, the Autumn Equinox coincides with the Sun's entrance into the Zodiac sign of Libra. Libra's symbol is the scales, and it is the sign known for seeking balance, harmony, and equality. However much some of us may prefer warmth to cold or light to dark (or vice versa), we know that without their opposites, we couldn't truly appreciate our favorite times of year. Participating in the turning of the Wheel through ritual and celebration helps us live in harmony with these shifting tides.

This recognition of the necessity of change—more specifically, the necessity of death in the cycle of life, death, and rebirth—is seen in the shifting relationship between the Goddess and the God. At Mabon, neither is young anymore. The aging God is even further weakened than at Lammas and will soon give way completely to the dominance of the dark at Samhain. The Goddess is still in her Mother aspect as the Earth continues to bear fruit. She still holds the new God in her womb, yet she is moving toward her Crone aspect as well, where she will reign alone over the dark, mysterious nights until the God is reborn at Yule.

The Goddess embodies the bittersweet quality of this time of year, as she mourns the passing of the God yet knows he will return anew. In some traditions, the Goddess follows the God to the Underworld, which is why the Earth becomes cold and barren. In others, it is her sadness at his absence that causes the leaves to fall, the plants to die, and the animals to slumber away in hidden shelters. Still others view the coming weeks simply as a time of needed rest for all of the Earth, the equal and balanced opposite of the active energy of Spring.

The Horn of Plenty

While the Autumn Equinox was celebrated in several places throughout Asia, there's little evidence to suggest that the ancient pagans of Europe marked this specific day with any major fanfare. However, harvest festivals were widely observed at some point during the fall season in many cultures. In the areas comprising what is now the United Kingdom, the traditional harvest festival was tied to both the solar and lunar calendars and held around the Full Moon closest to the Autumn Equinox. The remains of ancient Neolithic sites throughout Britain and Ireland that were designed to align with the Sun on this day show that it was considered an important moment to observe and honor.

This lack of historical information made the Autumn Equinox somewhat difficult to name, at least compared to the other solar Sabbats. In the early 1970s, Aidan Kelly, a prominent member of the growing Pagan community in the United States (see page 6), suggested that the holiday be called Mabon. Mabon ap Modron is the name of a Welsh mythological figure who is mentioned in the Mabinogion, the early Welsh prose stories, as well as in Arthurian legend. Some consider him a deity, but not enough is known about him to confirm this status, as many figures in ancient pagan myths are the children of unions between deities and humans. Nonetheless, Mabon is the son of the goddess Modron, who is often described as the primordial triple goddess of the ancient Celts. The story we have of Mabon is that he was abducted from his mother when he was three days old and imprisoned in a secret location into adulthood until King Arthur's men rescued him.

Mabon means "son," and Modron means "mother" in Welsh (Mabon ap Modron, son of the mother), so we don't really know whether these two mythical figures had specific names. However, these archetypes are somewhat fitting for a Wiccan Sabbat in that they echo the mother–child relationship of the Goddess and God.

As the mythology and symbolism of the Wheel of the Year has evolved, the tale of Mabon has grown into something new, with various writers borrowing elements of ancient myths from other cultures, especially the Greeks and the Norse. In one version, Modron's grief over her missing son is given as the reason for the turning of the season—her sadness causes darkness and cold to envelop the Earth. In another, it is Mabon's imprisonment deep within the ground that leads animals and plant life to turn inward. As with Ostara, we can see that the lore around Mabon is more modern than that of most other Sabbats. Nonetheless, the sorrow inherent to the original tale is appropriate for this time of year, as the absence of light looms closer and closer.

If Ostara's symbols are the hare and the egg, then the chief symbol of Mabon is the cornucopia, also known as the horn of plenty. This image—a large, hollowed-out horn overflowing with fruits and vegetables—is widely recognized in North America as part of the modern "harvest festival" of Thanksgiving. However, it was part of European harvest festivals for many centuries before making its way to the New World.

The word *cornucopia* comes from the Latin words for "horn" and "plenty," but the symbol itself goes back even further to the

ancient Greeks. It features prom-
inently in Greek mythology, particularly in a story about Zeus
as an infant. His supernatural
strength caused him to acciden-
tally break off one of the horns of
Amalthea, the goat who watched
over him and fed him with her

milk. The severed horn then gained the power to provide infinite
nourishment.

Other deities associated with the cornucopia include the Greek
goddesses Gaia (the Earth) and Demeter (a grain goddess) and the
Roman goddess Abundantia (the personification of abundance).
As we can see, the cornucopia is a very fitting symbol for this
Wiccan Sabbat—not just because of its pagan origins, but also
because of its association with the Horned God.

Celebrating Mabon

The cornucopia is an excellent place to start when it comes to
your Mabon celebration. You can make your own completely from
scratch or buy a horn-shaped basket and fill it with fresh autumn
produce, nuts, herbs, flowers and even crystals to place on your
altar. Use it in ritual to express gratitude for the abundance in your
life or in spellwork for abundance and prosperity. You can leave
it outdoors at night as an offering to the animals and faeries, and
bury whatever isn't eaten by the end of the following day. The cornucopia also makes an excellent gift and a way for you to share the
bounty in your life with others.

Coven rituals at Mabon often focus on balance and on giving
thanks for life's blessings, particularly those that have come
to pass over the past several months. You may identify new or

ongoing goals for the next and final harvest at Samhain. The Mabon feast is particularly lavish as we are at the height of the harvest season. Food is often shared with shelters and other organizations on behalf of the less fortunate.

There is also an acknowledgment of the coming dark, with thanks given to the retreating Sun. In some traditions, it is time to actively welcome the dark and to honor spirits and aging deities—especially Crone goddesses—in preparation for Samhain.

For Witches who tend gardens, now is the time to harvest what is ready, tend what is still growing, and collect and save seeds for next year's crops. You might make an offering to Nature spirits with some of your bounty, or offer seeds, grains and acorns, or cider.

Be sure to spend quality time outdoors, drinking in the last of the sunshine. Gather brightly colored leaves to place on your altar, and give thanks to the Goddess and God for the graceful beauty with which they bring the light half of the year to a close. For spellwork, consider goals related to harmony and balance, as well as protection, prosperity, and self-confidence.

Mabon Correspondences

COLORS: Deep reds, maroon, orange, yellow, gold, bronze, brown

STONES: Amber, topaz, citrine, tiger's eye, lapis lazuli, sapphire, yellow agate

HERBS: Chamomile, milkweed, thistle, yarrow, saffron, hops, Solomon's seal, sage, rue, hazel, ivy, oakmoss, mace

FLOWERS: Marigold, sunflower, rose, aster, chrysanthemum

INCENSE: Benzoin, cedar, pine, myrrh, frankincense, sandalwood, cinnamon, clove, sage

ALTAR DECORATIONS/SYMBOLS: Cornucopia, gourds, acorns, pine cones, pinwheels, yellow discs, other solar symbols and imagery

FOODS: Nuts, wheat and other grains, bread, grapes, apples, pumpkin, pomegranate, all autumn fruits and vegetables, wine

MABON FLOATING CANDLE SPELL

Mabon, like its "twin" Ostara, is a time to reflect on harmony and balance, but whereas the Spring Equinox focuses on balance in your relationship with the outer world, the Autumn Equinox asks you to turn your focus inward. What aspects of your relationship with yourself could use some balancing? Are you open and listening to your own inner guidance, or are you letting the opinions of others get in the way? Are you speaking kindly to and about yourself, or are you always being your own harshest critic? What nagging thoughts or emotions might you be in the habit of ignoring or stuffing down?

Traditionally, Autumn is associated with the Element of Water, which rules the psychic and emotional tides that ebb and flow between our conscious and unconscious selves. This spell evokes the theme of balance with a candle floating in a cauldron. Use the spell as a portal to strengthen your inner balance for the coming season and as a way of preparing for any shadow work you'd like to take on at Samhain.

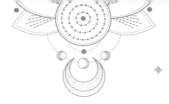

1 work candle for atmosphere
Small cauldron or bowl
Marigold or sunflower petals
1 white floating candle
Pen (or pencil) and journal

≡ INSTRUCTIONS ≡

Light the work candle. Fill the cauldron with water up to about ½ inch (1 cm) from the top. Sprinkle the flower petals on the water's surface and gently float the candle among the petals.

Spend some time journaling about any inner conflicts or questions you'd like to harmonize within yourself. Try to write for at least 20 minutes. When you feel you've hit on a particular aspect of yourself that could use some balancing at this time, write a short phrase or draw a symbol that represents it.

Light the floating candle as you keep this phrase or symbol in your mind. Sit quietly for a few moments and take in the sight of the flame, water, and petals. You may wish to resume writing or stay open for any insights that come to you regarding your issue. Leave the candle to burn out on its own, under supervision.

AUTUMN PROTECTION CHARM

This charm can be used at any time of year, but it's especially appropriate for Autumn when the impending darkness can start to get under your skin. Keep negativity at bay with this combination of herbs and minerals from the Earth. Each of the stones and herbs below are used in protection magic. You can use any combination of the herbs and crystals listed here. Select those that resonate with you most for a personalized charm. For optimal protective powers, use at least two of the three herbs.

YOU WILL NEED

1 or 2 pieces of tiger's eye, amber, and/or carnelian

1 tablespoon dried sage

1 tablespoon dried chamomile

1 tablespoon dried yarrow

Small drawstring bag

INSTRUCTIONS

Charge the stones and herbs in direct sunlight for one hour. Place the charged ingredients in the drawstring bag and visualize yourself surrounded by golden light as you are doing so. Carry the charm with you whenever you feel highly energetically sensitive.

⟪ S A M H A I N ⟫

PRONUNCIATION: *SOW-in*, *SAH-vin*, or *SOW-een*

THEMES: Death, rebirth, divination, honoring ancestors, introspection, benign mischief, revelry

ALSO KNOWN AS: Samhuin, Oidhche Shamhna, Halloween, Third Harvest, Day of the Dead, Félie Na Marbh (Feast of the Dead), Shadowfest, Ancestor Night, Feile Moingfinne (Snow Goddess), Winter Nights, Old Hallowmas, Calan Gaeaf

Of all the Sabbats, Samhain is considered to be the most powerful and important to Wiccans and other Witches, with many intense energies at play. This is when we honor the Death element of the life/death/rebirth cycle that forms the basis of the Wheel of the Year and all of Nature as we know it.

Wiccans understand that death is the most potent part of the cycle, as it is here that all potential for new life resides, waiting to be manifested into specific form. Therefore, Samhain is the most fitting time for reflection. It is ideal for looking back over the past year to identify any circumstances or patterns of behavior we would like to allow to die so that we can make room for the new when the growing season begins again. By letting go of our old selves, we can move into the Winter months ahead with clarity and acceptance of the ever-turning wheel of life and death.

The name Samhain has been translated from the Old Irish as "Summer's end," and this date marked the beginning of the dark half of the year in the ancient Celtic world. This is the third and final harvest festival, the time to stock the root cellars with the last of the winter squashes, turnips, beets, and other root vegetables, and to dry the last of the magical and medicinal herbs for winter storage.

The fields are now empty of their crops, the once-green meadow grasses are dying back, turning to gold and brown. The leaves have peaked and fallen, leaving the trees bare and stark against the graying skies. The chill in the air that began with Mabon is now here to stay, and the weakened Sun gives barely a passing glance for a few short hours before descending again below the horizon. It can seem as if the world is dying at this time, but we alleviate this feeling by expressing gratitude for all the abundance of the past year and knowing that the light will return, as the Wheel promises.

The God and Goddess enact the perpetual cycle of life, death, and rebirth at Samhain. In his Sun aspect, the God has aged considerably since Mabon. His power is nearly gone, and he descends into the Underworld, leaving the Earth to the darkness of Winter. As the Horned God, or the God of the Hunt, he is a fully mature stag who gives his life so his people can survive the coming barren season. Wiccans say farewell to the God at this Sabbat, thanking him for fulfilling his life-sustaining roles over the past year and expressing faith that he will return, reborn, at Yule.

In many traditions, the Goddess is said to be mourning the God at this time, yet she too knows that he will return, as she is now in her wise Crone aspect. From the aged Crone, we learn that death is part of life, that the old must be released for us to learn, grow, and birth new manifestations. It is interesting that the Goddess herself never dies, since the Earth remains steadily present throughout the year, no matter where the Sun may be, yet she represents death and life simultaneously. She is both the Crone and mother-to-be of the new God.

Spirits and Symbols

For the Celts, from whom the name and many customs of this Sabbat are borrowed, Samhain was something of a dark mirror to Beltane—a counterpart that sits directly opposite to Beltane on the Wheel.

Samhain was yet another time to move cattle, only now they were brought to their winter pastures. The ritual bonfires and great gatherings that celebrated fertility in May were now a recognition of the abundance manifested throughout the light half of the year. This was the time to gather the last harvest of apples and nuts and to select the animals that would be slaughtered to feed the people for the coming months. The meat would be salted and stored for the Winter, and the bones from the Samhain feast were thrown upon the fires as offerings to secure good fortune for the next season's cattle. (This tradition gives us the word *bonfire*—a combination of *bone* and *fire*.)

The gatherings at Samhain were festive affairs, as people danced, drank, feasted, and traded goods for the last time before Winter kept everyone close to home. It was an important time, especially as many key tales in early Irish mythology occur at Samhain, such as the *Táin Bó Cúailnge* (*The Cattle Raid of Cooley*).

As the first day of Winter and the beginning of the dark half of the year, Samhain was, like its Beltane counterpart, a time of open passageways between the world of the living and the Otherworld, or world of the spirit. However, whereas Beltane focused on Summer and the bursting forth of life that warmth and sunshine bring, Samhain acknowledged the cold, the dying back of the Earth, and the dead who have gone before us.

Samhain Eve, like Beltane Eve, was also a time of heightened activity from the aos sí, or faeries, who were said to be extra mischievous now. People steered clear of these supernatural beings and even avoided being outdoors on this night. If they had to leave home, they would carry iron or salt to discourage the aos sí from coming near. They believed that the aos sí needed to be appeased as well, in order to ensure that the family and its livestock survived the coming Winter, so many families left offerings of food and drink for the faeries outside the door of the house.

With the Otherworld so easily accessible, Samhain was seen as an occasion for honoring the dead, who were thought to wander about and visit their family homes, seeking a warm welcome and a meal. The Samhain feast always included a place at the table reserved for the ancestors, and celebrants left room for them by the hearth in their homes. To make sure their loved ones could find their way, they lit a single candle in each window of the house. People also left apples along the roadsides for spirits who had no living relatives to welcome them.

In general, it was believed that the dead, like the aos sí, had to be appeased at this time or misfortune might fall upon the family. However, appreciative departed souls could bestow blessings as well. Many ancient cultures around the world share this belief in the need to placate the dead, and it is seen most explicitly today in the Mexican holiday Día de los Muertos (Day of the Dead), which begins on October 31 and has roots in both European and Aztec cultures.

Since the spirit world was so readily accessible at Samhain, divination was a popular activity during the festival. Many different forms were practiced, often to discover information about future marriages or deaths. People's names were marked on stones, which were then thrown into the bonfire. The stones would be plucked from the ashes the next day, and the condition they were in would inform how they were "read."

Crows and other birds were counted as they passed in the sky, with their number or direction being assigned specific meanings. Apples and nuts were often used in divination games. One popular activity involved removing the peel of an apple in one unbroken strip, casting the peel onto the floor, and seeing what letter of the alphabet the shape formed. The letter that appeared would be the first initial of your future spouse's name. Another tradition involving the fruit evolved into what we now know as bobbing for apples. The first person to successfully retrieve an apple with their teeth was said to be the next to marry. In Celtic mythology, the apple was associated with immortality and the Otherworld. In Scottish myths, Druids chewed hazelnuts, which were associated with divine wisdom, to gain prophecies.

There are many aspects of our modern Halloween celebrations that have their roots in Samhain customs. The fear of faeries and spirits roaming the night led our Celtic ancestors to disguise themselves in white so they could blend in with the ghosts. Some wore costumes made of straw to confuse them. This evolved into the tradition of "guising," in which people dressed in disguise to represent the spirits of the night and traveled from house to house collecting gifts of apples, nuts, and other food for the Samhain feast.

In Scotland, it was common for those imitating the mischievous faeries to play pranks on their neighbors, especially if they did not receive an offering from the household. These original "trick-or-treaters" carried lanterns made from hollowed-out turnips, which were often carved with frightening faces to represent or ward off evil spirits. The lanterns were also left on windowsills or doorsteps to protect the home on Samhain Eve, a custom that later evolved into carving our modern jack-o'-lanterns.

Other symbols of Halloween that may have originated with the Celts include the skull and the skeleton. Celtic warriors revered the skull as the house of the soul and the seat of one's power, and it is thought that skulls were used as oracles.

A classic symbol of Halloween is, of course, the Witch and all of her associated imagery—the broom, the cauldron, and the black cat. This link stems from the misguided fear of "evil witches" promoted by the Christian churches in later centuries, and thus the stereotypical Witch is lumped in with vampires, goblins, and other supernatural creatures each Halloween season. Nonetheless, Witchcraft is a practice that invites cooperation from the spirit world in a variety of ways, so the archetypal Witch can be seen as a fitting symbol for both holidays. There's a nice bit of irony in that Samhain—the "Witch's holiday"—seems to be the one that the Church just couldn't stamp out entirely. Although November 1 was converted to All Saints' Day, the old pagan trappings of the original festival remain alive and well, even in mainstream culture.

CELEBRATING SAMHAIN

For Wiccans and other Pagans, Samhain is very much rooted in ancient Celtic traditions. This is the time between death and new life, as the Crone/Mother Goddess waits for the God to be reborn, and it is often described as the night when "the veil between the worlds is at its thinnest." Many choose to honor their ancestors and other departed loved ones at this time. Food and drink are left out for any wandering spirits, and many Witches seek communication with the Other Side.

We do not fear mischief or retribution from the dead, as we know our ancestors don't mean us harm. We honor and respect their presence. Wiccans also mediate upon the belief in reincarnation at Samhain, as we recognize that the cycle of life, death, and rebirth applies to all living beings. We know that we do not return to the Other Side permanently, but rest and enjoy ourselves there until we're ready to be reborn into the physical world.

Samhain is a key occasion for divination of all kinds, including scrying, Tarot, runes, and I-Ching, as well as various uses of apples. For those who work with the faeries, this is an important night to leave offerings for them!

In many traditions, Samhain is also considered the start of the new year, as it is believed that the Celtic year began on the evening of October 31. Scholars disagree about whether there is sufficient evidence for this, but Samhain is listed in Irish medieval literature as the first of the four cross-quarter day festivals, so the association has stuck. Whether your tradition considers the year to begin now or at Yule, Samhain is an excellent time to reflect on your life and any changes you wish to make during the year ahead. What in your personal world do you wish to allow to die, and what new developments would you like to give birth to? What has ended that you need to fully let go of in order to make room for the new?

Coven rituals at Samhain are often held outdoors at night, around a sacred bonfire. The coven members may focus on letting go of bad habits and other unwanted energies, symbolically releasing them into the fire to be transformed. Other ritual themes may include bidding farewell to the Old God, tapping into the wisdom of the Crone, and formally honoring the dead.

Any Wiccans who practice spellwork are certain to do so on this night, the most potent time of the entire year for magic. Spellwork practiced at this time is bound to be effective, but in keeping with the themes of this Sabbat, goals related to banishing, releasing, and strengthening your psychic abilities are especially appropriate.

On your Samhain altar, include photographs or mementos from deceased loved ones and light a votive candle specifically for them. Since this is the Sabbat most associated with Witchcraft, include symbols like cauldrons, besoms (ritual brooms), and pentacles, even if you don't work with these tools regularly. As always, seasonal decorations of all kinds are key, but try to include a pumpkin if you can—carved and illuminated, if possible.

Finally, be sure to give your sacred space a very thorough sweeping before beginning any ritual or spellwork. As you clean, visualize all unwanted energies and influences from the past year being swept away and out of your life.

Samhain Correspondences

COLORS: Black, orange, rust, bronze, brown, gray, silver, gold

STONES: Jet, obsidian, onyx, smoky quartz, all other black stones, bloodstone, carnelian

HERBS: Mugwort, wormwood, valerian, rosemary, sage, catnip, broom, oak leaves, witch hazel, angelica

FLOWERS: Marigold, chrysanthemums, sunflower, goldenrod, Russian sage, pansies

INCENSE: Nutmeg, mint, sage, copal, myrrh, clove, heather, heliotrope, benzoin, sweetgrass, sandalwood

ALTAR DECORATIONS/SYMBOLS: Oak leaves and other fallen leaves, pomegranates, pumpkins, squashes, gourds, photos or other tokens of deceased loved ones, acorns, flint corn, besom, cauldron

FOODS: Pumpkins, pomegranates, apples, all root vegetables and winter squashes, all nuts, breads, beans, apple cider, mulled cider, ale, herbal teas

SPELL FOR BURNING AWAY BAD HABITS

With its emphasis on banishing and the death of the old, Samhain is a perfect opportunity to get some magical assistance with releasing any habit you want to be free of. The only caveat is that you have to *want* to end the habit. Without that motivation, this spell is unlikely to succeed.

1 work candle for atmosphere (optional)

5 pieces of jet, obsidian, onyx, smoky quartz,
and/or black tourmaline

Cauldron or other heatproof dish

1 black candle

Small square of paper

Pen or pencil (or ink and quill)

≡ INSTRUCTIONS ≡

Light the work candle, if using. Arrange the stones around the cauldron in a pentagram shape. Light the black candle and sit quietly, imagining the freedom and vitality you will experience with this habit gone from your life. When you're ready, write the habit on the square of paper. Holding it in your dominant hand, raise it over the candle flame and say the following (or similar) words:

"As the fire burns among these stones
I ask the blessings of the Crone:
Release this habit written here
without judgment, without fear."

Now ignite the paper with the flame. (Be careful not to burn your fingers!) When it's burning enough to incinerate completely, drop it into the cauldron. Take the ashes outside and sprinkle them onto the Earth.

Allow the candle to burn out on its own, under supervision. Bury the stones or throw them into a creek or river to cast away all remaining traces of the habit.

SPIRIT-GUIDED WRITING

Spirit-guided writing, also known as automatic writing, is a very effective way to channel insights and advice from the spirit realm. Each of us has guides on the Other Side with wisdom to share if we tap into their energies. If you write in a journal regularly, you have most likely already received information from the spirit world in the form of inspired thoughts that seem to flow out of the pen without effort. Automatic writing is similar, but in this case, you're deliberately asking for the words to come through you, without your conscious mind making any decisions about the content or otherwise interfering in the process.

If writing at your altar isn't practical, transform a desk or table into your sacred space for this work. Be sure to ground and center yourself by meditating, taking a ritual bath, or any other activity that helps you connect with your highest energy. Opening yourself up to spirit energy can be disorienting and even unpleasant if you're not properly grounded, so it's especially important to prepare yourself energetically before you begin. **Note: This spell includes mugwort; avoid using mugwort while pregnant or breastfeeding. You can substitute it with bay leaf, honeysuckle flower, or star anise, if needed.**

≡ YOU WILL NEED ≡

1 white candle

1 quartz crystal

1 amethyst

Sage bundle

Dried mugwort, bay leaf, honeysuckle, or star anise

Journal or sheets of writing paper

Pen or pencil

Light the candle, and place the quartz and amethyst on either side of it. Use the flame to ignite the sage bundle, and smudge yourself and your surroundings to clear away any unwanted energy. Take a few deep breaths and say the following (or similar) words:

"I surround myself in love and light
and seek my spirits' guidance tonight.
Guardians wise and helpers sage,
speak truth to me through pen and page."

To prime the psychic connection between you and your guides, gently rub mugwort over the front and back of your journal (or on the first and last sheets of paper). Then take up your pen (or pencil) and begin writing whatever comes to mind. It may take a little while before your conscious mind lets go and the words begin to feel that they're coming from outside of you. If you like, you can write down a question to get started, but don't be surprised if what comes through is on a different topic altogether—you're asking for what the Universe most wants you to know at this time.

Write for at least 10 to 15 minutes. Remember, don't pay conscious attention to what you're writing—instead, let your eyes focus softly on your hand, your pen, or the candle as you let the automatic writing take over. When you're ready to stop, set the

pen down, shake out both of your hands, and then read what you've written. Gently extinguish the candle when you're through. You may want to save the pages and return to them a few weeks or months down the road to see how the messages fit with your life as it's unfolding.

PART THREE

MOON MAGIC

THE POWER OF THE DIVINE FEMININE

ONE OF THE MANY ASPECTS THAT MAKES WICCA UNIQUE among modern religions is its elevation of the divine feminine. In contrast to the Abrahamic religions, in which God is only masculine, traditional Wiccan belief recognizes divinity as both masculine and feminine, with the God and Goddess being present in all of Nature.

Both deities are honored at the Sabbats, but it is the God, in his role as the Sun, whose cyclical journey is the focus of the story of the Wheel. The Goddess, as the embodiment of Earth, has an equal role within the overall Sabbat story, but the changes taking place from season to season—from life to death to rebirth, from planting to growth to harvest—are a result of the God's presence or absence.

In contrast, the Esbats focus solely on the Goddess, in her role as the Moon, and her triple aspects of Maiden, Mother and Crone. Her continual transformation from one aspect to another in a never-ending cycle mirrors the ever-shifting Moon itself and reminds us of the impermanent yet eternal nature of our existence as souls transforming from one life to the next.

As a celestial body that can be seen both at night and during the day, the Moon is the quintessential traveler between the worlds—of light and dark, seen and unseen, physical and spiritual. The divine light of the Goddess emanates from the Moon, and it can be felt in any moment of quiet reflection and attunement to lunar energy.

Many sources on Wicca and Paganism emphasize the New Moon and Full Moon, and understandably so, but this can leave the impression that the Moon's significance is limited to these times. However, each phase of the lunar cycle presents opportunities for spiritual connection and successful magic. This is because each phase offers particular energies that you can attune with, reflect on, and harness for your specific magical goals.

Indeed, getting to know the Moon and its energy will deepen your experience of the Esbats and take your understanding of magic to a new level. The following pages will introduce you to the lunar phases in detail, as well as their correspondences to the three aspects of the Triple Moon Goddess. We'll also take a look at the Esbats and the Triple Goddess herself, the effects of lunar energy on animals and humans, and how to work magic with the entire lunar cycle.

The Esbats and the Triple Moon Goddess

While the term "Wheel of the Year" is commonly understood to refer to the eight Sabbats, in practice it also includes the Esbats. In some traditions, these are known as the "minor Sabbats." The Esbats comprise an inner wheel that rotates alongside the outer wheel of the Sabbats but at a slightly faster pace. They occur either twelve or thirteen times per year, depending on how the lunar calendar lines up with the Gregorian calendar. Esbats are typically held at each Full Moon (though some covens meet at the New Moon instead).

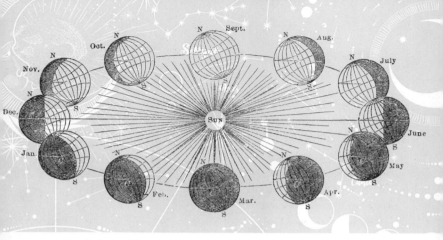

As with the Sabbats, the details of the Esbat rituals vary widely among covens and solitary Wiccans. Magical goals often include individual intentions as well as communal and even global needs, such as healing, abundance, and respect for the Earth and her natural resources. Very often, the focus of the rituals will align with the time of year or honor a specific aspect of the Goddess. For example, an Esbat taking place in late Autumn may be devoted to a Crone goddess such as Kali (Hindu) or Badb (Celtic), while a Spring Esbat might focus on Maiden goddesses like Diana (Greek) or Ostara (Anglo-Saxon).

In Wiccan cosmology, the Moon is the ultimate symbol of the Goddess, the all-encompassing divine feminine. In her three-fold form of Maiden, Mother, and Crone is the embodiment of divine lunar energy. The Goddess *is* the Moon, and her ever-shifting forms symbolize the transformative power available in magic. While she is usually honored with Esbats at the Full Moon, which corresponds to her Mother aspect, all three aspects are equally relevant when you are attuning with the rhythms of Nature and viewing each day through a magical lens.

The Maiden

The Maiden aspect of the Triple Goddess emerges with the crescent Moon and reigns during the waxing days as the Moon becomes full. She represents the youth and innocence of life before motherhood, and so is associated with all things "new": the dawn, the sunrise, the Spring, young animals, and all that is ripening into fullness. The Maiden assists with activities involving creativity, beauty, exploration, self-discovery, and self-expression. She supports the characteristics of self-confidence, intelligence, and independence. Magically, she assists with goals related to new beginnings, romance, and partnerships. Goddesses who typically represent the Maiden include the Greek goddesses Persephone and Artemis, the Celtic Rhiannon, the Nordic Freya, and many others from around the globe.

The Mother

The Mother Goddess is aligned with the days just before, during, and after the Full Moon. Having matured from Maiden to Mother, her time is the afternoon, when the day's light is at its strongest. Her season is the lush full swing of Summer. As the one who brings forth new life, she is the goddess most associated with manifestation of all kinds as well as adulthood, responsibility, and tending and nurturing what has come into being. As the symbol of the Full Moon, she is often revered as the most powerful of the three aspects of the Triple Goddess. Her energy supports magical work related to abundance, good health, self-care, and reaping rewards for your past efforts. The Mother is often worshipped in the guise of the Roman goddess Ceres, the Greek Demeter and Selene, and the Celtic Badb and Danu, among others.

The Crone

As the Moon wanes, becoming less visible with each passing day, the Crone steps into her power. The most mysterious of the three aspects, she is associated with sunset and night, and Autumn and Winter—the darkest times in the cycle of life and death on Earth. Finished now with the duties of motherhood, the Goddess turns her focus to the domains of death and ultimate rebirth. Her understanding of these cycles makes her the wise elder. She supports experiences involving aging, completions, prophecies and visions, transformation, and death—both literal and figurative. The Crone reigns during the dark of the Moon, patiently tending the nights until the New Moon returns. Call on her for assistance with magic related to strength, healing, banishing, and removing obstacles. She is represented by a wide range of goddesses, including the Russian Baba Yaga, the Greek Hecate, and the Celtic Morrigan and Cailleach Bear.

Like the Sabbats, which mark distinct seasonal points on the Wheel, each Full Moon has its own distinct seasonal energy. For example, the Full Moons of late Summer and Autumn tend to have a more electric feeling than the quiet, more subtle energies of Winter Moons. Each Full Moon also has its own name, which generally honors an aspect of the natural world, agricultural cycles, animal behavior, and even human activities. There are several names for each Moon, which are borrowed from various Native American traditions, the ancient Celts and, more rarely, Chinese traditions. For example, the Full Moon in January is known as the Ice Moon, the Wolf Moon, or the Stay Home Moon. The most commonly used names in Wiccan traditions are noted on the table on the facing page.

FULL MOON
MONTHS AND NAMES

MONTH	MOON NAME
JANUARY	Cold Moon (also Hunger Moon)
FEBRUARY	Quickening Moon (also Snow Moon)
MARCH	Storm Moon (also Sap Moon)
APRIL	Wind Moon (also Pink Moon)
MAY	Flower Moon (also Milk Moon)
JUNE	Sun Moon (also Strong Sun Moon and Rose Moon)
JULY	Blessing Moon (also Thunder Moon)
AUGUST	Corn Moon (also Grain Moon)
SEPTEMBER	Harvest Moon
OCTOBER	Blood Moon
NOVEMBER	Mourning Moon (also Frost Moon)
DECEMBER	Long Nights Moon

Lunar Energy: Mystery and Magnetism

Just as our pagan ancestors ritually observed solar and agricultural cycles, it's evident that the Moon played an important role in many ancient belief systems. It was certainly not lost on those who lived near the oceans that the Moon has an effect on the tides and on the sea life they relied upon for sustenance. Likewise, hunters all over the planet would have noted behavioral patterns of animals that aligned with lunar cycles and planned their hunts accordingly. Agrarian cultures took the Moon into account as well and used it to determine the best times for planting and harvesting crops. The Moon's importance to the survival of our ancestors was just as significant as that of the Sun.

Moon worship is found in the oldest religious writings of ancient Egypt, Babylonia, China, and India, and deities from a wide variety of ancient cultures are associated with the Moon. In some traditions, the Moon's ever-repeating pattern of disappearing and reappearing was associated with concepts of life, death, and rebirth. Many agricultural societies saw the Moon as a female ruler of vegetation cycles. The concept of yin and yang energies in ancient Chinese philosophy ascribed the Moon to yin, or female energy, balancing out the yang energy of the Sun.

Just as the Earth has its own energy, which is independent from the energy it receives from the Sun, the Moon, too, emits an energy that is subtle yet distinctive. Many have described this power as magnetic, which makes sense to anyone who has felt "pulled" in some way by the Moon. Some particularly sensitive people feel a physical tug in their bodies at the Full or New Moon, while others just notice a heightened sense of awareness to everything in their environment.

Scientists have observed the effects of the Moon's cycles on animal behavior, particularly when it comes to mating and hunting. These effects occur in both nocturnal animals and animals primarily active during the day, and even show up in certain insects. Several species of birds change their communication patterns around the Full Moon. Even household pets appear to be affected—veterinary emergency rooms see an uptick in visits from cats and dogs on Full Moon nights.

Of course, humans are animals too, and as such, they are no less susceptible to the effects of the Moon's perpetual transformations. It has been noted since ancient times that women's menstrual cycles are often in rhythm with the Moon. Ovulation and conception rates are lower at the New Moon and tend to peak around the days leading up to and through the Full Moon. Furthermore, at least one study has shown that more births occur during times when the Moon is closest to the Earth, meaning that its gravitational pull is at its strongest. The Moon has also been shown to affect sleep patterns, and even the outcomes of surgery—people undergoing emergency heart surgery fare better during the days around the Full Moon than at other points in the Moon's cycle.

What science has not been able to prove so far is a phenomenon that is well known to many who work in various human service occupations: people just seem to get a little "loony" during the Full Moon. While no studies have confirmed that this is true, you can ask just about any bartender, child care worker, or emergency room attendant, and you'll hear tales of increased accidents, erratic behavior, and downright "moodiness" during these times. In fact, the word *lunatic*, rooted in *luna,* the Latin word for "moon," comes from the belief that changes in the Moon's appearance could cause temporary insanity.

Lunar energy is feminine and receptive, in contrast to the masculine, projective energy of the Sun. We can look directly at the Moon without hurting our eyes because the Moon actually reflects the projected light of the Sun, rather than projecting light itself. It's interesting that what we call the lunar cycle is actually a manifestation of shifting shadows caused by the Moon's journey around the Earth. Its phases are really a study in contrast between the

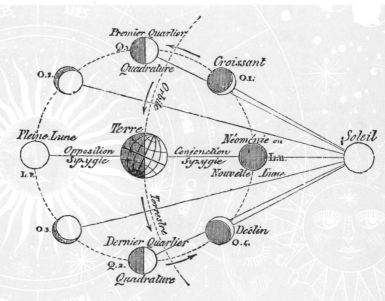

seen and unseen. Perhaps this is why the Moon appeals to the mysterious, psychic, and magical qualities within our human selves.

Indeed, the energy of the Moon—feminine, receptive, and magnetic—is tailor-made for interacting with the energy of our own intuition, which has the same qualities. When we consciously connect with lunar energy, we open our capacity to channel that energy into attracting what we desire to us and releasing what we don't want from our lives. When we do so in conscious harmony with the energetic rhythms of the Moon's cycle, we can amplify the power of our magical work.

Magical Timing and the Lunar Cycle

Generally speaking, the relationship between magic and the Moon can be summed up as follows: as the Moon grows, we work magic for increase; as it wanes, we work magic for decrease. Another way to think about it is that when you're seeking to bring something into your life, you work with the waxing Moon, and when you want to banish or release some unwanted element of your life, you work with the waning Moon.

The transition point between these two opposites is the Full Moon, a time of "harvest" as we celebrate what we have manifested over the first half of the cycle. We then "clean up" afterward, identifying and releasing what is no longer needed throughout the second half of the cycle. At the New Moon, we set new intentions for the next cycle of manifestation, and on and on it goes.

The rhythm of this cycle can be visualized as the rhythm of the tides, which the Moon causes. The waves grow bigger and come closer, covering more of the shoreline as the tide rises. The incoming surf peaks at high tide, and then recedes, exposing more and more shoreline until it reaches the low tide mark before it begins to rise again.

If you start paying close attention to how you think and feel during each phase of the cycle, you'll be better able to understand how these rhythms affect your personal power. You can use these discoveries to strengthen your magical abilities. To do this, you'll need to know where the Moon is in its cycle and (ideally) where and when it can be seen in the sky. If you're not accustomed to observing the Moon at this level of detail, the following information will help you start tracking the lunar cycle for yourself.

Light and Shadow: Following the Moon

There are two different frameworks for describing and tracking the Moon's orbit around the Earth. The first is based on its appearance in the sky. It begins as a barely detectable sliver at the New Moon. Over the next few days, the sliver becomes larger and more defined, almost resembling the tip of a fingernail. This is called the Crescent Moon. From here, the Moon continues to grow—or "wax"— on its way to becoming full. At the midpoint between new and full, we see the waxing Half Moon, with the illuminated half on the right and the shadowed half on the left. As the circle begins to be filled out with light, it becomes *gibbous*, a word used in astronomy to describe the bulging appearance of the Moon during the days just before and after it's completely full. Finally, when the circle is completely lit, we see the Full Moon.

In the days just after the full point, the Moon is gibbous again, then continues to shrink—or wane—until only half of it is illuminated. This time, the light half is on the left, with the shadowed half on the right. More and more of the Moon is covered in shadow as it wanes back to its crescent point, and then completely disappears. This window of time is the Dark Moon. Once the sliver returns, the cycle begins again.

Another way of tracking the Moon's cycle is to do so mathematically. The cycle is divided into four quarters, spread out

over roughly 28 days. Each quarter lasts approximately seven days, and adding up the four quarters creates what we call the lunar "month." The first quarter begins at the New Moon and ends at the waxing half. The second quarter runs from there until the Full Moon. The third quarter begins immediately after the Moon turns full and lasts until the waning Half Moon, and the fourth quarter closes out the cycle through the Dark Moon, ending just as the New Moon reemerges.

While these two systems don't conflict with each other when it comes to describing the full lunar cycle, they do not completely correspond. The ordered, even-numbered quarter system contains four units, which doesn't quite align with the five major marking points—New, Half, Full, Half, Dark—of the older, appearance-based framework. This is because the quarter system doesn't take the Dark Moon period into account. In reality, the Moon takes 29.5 days to complete its orbit, so there's a slight lag in the pace between the fourth and first quarters when the Moon is dark.

The quarter system is also somewhat rigid in the context of magic. For example, the period of amplified energetic influence that the Full Moon exerts is much longer than the brief period of time when it's fully illuminated. In the Witching world, the Full Moon phase is considered to be five days long—from the two days before Full, when the Moon is still gibbous, until two days after, when the waning is just becoming visible. (Some even designate a full week to the Full Moon!) For the purposes of working with lunar energies, it can be argued that the Full Moon phase begins and ends when you *feel* it beginning and ending. To some extent, the entire lunar cycle can be seen through this lens. Remember, magic is ultimately about your personal intuitive perception—your sixth sense.

It doesn't matter which system you work with, as long as you're aware of when the New and Full Moons occur. These are, after all, the two most energetically powerful times of the cycle, so if you're new to paying close attention to the Moon, start by closely observing these two points. As you practice this for a few months, you'll find yourself attuning to the subtler, continuous rhythms of the Moon's energies throughout its cycle. You'll also get a better feel for timing your magic to align as closely as possible with each lunar phase.

THE MOON'S JOURNEY

Now we'll examine each phase of the lunar cycle in detail, with an eye for how the energies of each phase can help you shape your magic. This overview describes how the energies operate over the course of the cycle, which can be applied to a single magical goal identified at the New Moon and worked for over the next four weeks. Of course, in practice, this time frame is too short for many intentions, but the purpose here is to illustrate the possibilities for being deliberate with your magical timing and how you can choose specific angles from which to approach the goal according to the current lunar phase.

New Moon

The New Moon marks the beginning of the lunar cycle. After a period of darkness, with no source of light in the night sky, the tiniest sliver of the Moon's surface emerges. It's not yet big enough to be visible to the naked eye, but it can still be felt energetically by many who are attuned to lunar rhythms.

This is a good time for dreaming of what you wish to create in your life. Perhaps you don't know exactly what you want it to look like, but taking some time to imagine how you will feel once it has manifested will guide you toward a more specific vision as the month goes on. For example, if you want to get a new job but don't have a clear sense of where or in what field you'd like to work, use the New Moon as a time to open up to various possibilities, including those you haven't consciously thought of. Listen to your intuition and see which ones feel the most alive to you. Work a spell that asks for help in clarifying your employment goals, or invite a number of potential offers to come your way so you can make decisions from a highly empowered place.

Traditionally, magic aimed at initiating new projects and ventures is favored at this time, but anything that involves attracting or increasing what you desire is appropriate. It's also a good time for formalizing any intentions around self-improvement, such as developing an exercise plan or creating a resolution to learn more about a particular topic. Keep in mind that New Moon spells aren't really about *instant* manifestation. They're about new beginnings, initiating actions that will bear fruit down the road. We plant the seeds, water them gently, and remain patient as they begin to germinate.

Many Witches work their spells as close as possible to the exact time of the New Moon, or just after, as this is thought to be the most potent time to harness the magical energies of this phase. Others prefer to cast New Moon spells during daylight hours, since the Moon rises and sets with the Sun at this point in the cycle. If you do not have the luxury of doing either, don't let it worry you. Just do your best to work on the actual day (or night) of the New Moon or no more than one day after, if you want to align your work with these particular energies.

GODDESSES: Diana (Roman), Artemis (Greek), Astarte (Phoenician)

Waxing Crescent

Beginning with the day after the New Moon and over the next few days, the Crescent Moon becomes more and more noticeable in the sky. The crescent is a symbol of the Triple Goddess, envisioned by

Wiccans as the shining cup of her hand, holding within her palm the potential of the Universe. The Goddess is coming into her Maiden role at this time, her youthful energy full of the promise of blessings to come.

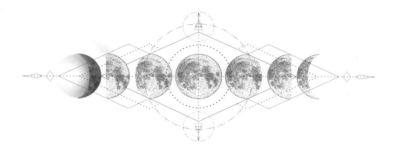

This phase is the ideal time for taking action on the physical plane that moves you toward the goals you've intended to achieve on the spiritual plane. The lunar energy at this time supports the beginning of forward movement. This can mean taking relatively small steps, such as establishing a routine of checking job listings or contacting people you know can assist you with whatever it is you're seeking to manifest. Be willing to meet new people and vary your usual routine in order to allow new possibilities to come into your awareness. Watch for opportunities related to your goal to show up during this time, and be sure to take advantage of them, as doing so confirms to the Universe that you truly want what you are working toward. This is how we root our manifestations—by taking the individual steps toward our goal as they present themselves.

Magic during the Crescent Moon is related to attraction and increase, but the energy begins to pick up the pace and move things into a somewhat more defined focus. It is time to revisit the seed of intention you planted at the New Moon and evaluate how it may be taking shape. Work spells to strengthen your resolve to see things through and to draw even more assistance from the Universe in the days to come. Spellwork regarding creativity, business, and financial matters is favored, as this is a fortuitous time to begin new ventures and step out into the unknown. Truly, anything you wish to draw to you is a good area of focus now. If you have many inspired ideas and are unsure where to start, sit with each one and tune into your intuition. You can also ask the Maiden for guidance in selecting and focusing on your goal. Those who like to work when the Moon is up can cast spells from midmorning until the hour after sundown.

GODDESSES: All Maiden goddesses, such as Aphrodite (Greek), Aine (Irish), and Idunn (Norse)

Waxing Half

Continuing its outward expansion, the Moon finishes its first quarter and reaches the midpoint between New and Full. There is a somewhat more fiery aspect to the energy here as the pace of growth quickens and activities are ramping up. This energy can be harnessed for any goals that involve people coming together to create something new or enhance an existing creation. Alternatively, you may find yourself in more consistent cocreation with the Universe itself, discovering your "groove" as you continue to allow new opportunities related to your goals to flow into your experience.

It's an ideal time to begin building the infrastructure related to your magical goals, whether this means creating more detailed plans, following through on initial opportunities, or gathering support from those who can be of assistance. There is a heightened emphasis on growth and nurturing your newly sprouted intention. You can look for ways to harness the increasing push of energy coming from the Moon to fuel your progress.

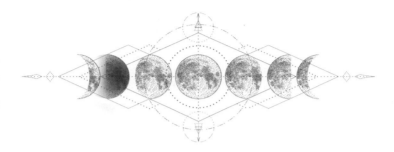

If you're not encountering any evidence of manifestation yet, there may be various factors at play. Are you staying in touch with your intuition and paying attention to subtle nudges from the Universe? Are unexpected circumstances or changes occurring in your daily life? Remember that sometimes, occurrences that seem inconvenient or annoying in the moment turn out to be steps on the path to realizing a goal, though we have no way of knowing that in the moment. Do your best to be at peace and trust the Universe to work out the "how" and the "when" of your manifestation. If you are attached to specific expectations, you may be blocking what you desire from coming into your life.

Magical work at the waxing Half Moon is generally related to gaining or strengthening partnerships with others, such as friends, romantic interests, or business associates. Improving physical health and general well-being is also favored now. You may also feel guided to "boost" any spellwork begun at the New Moon, perhaps by lighting a candle to add new energy to the existing working, creating a luck charm with your goal in mind, or simply by visualizing the manifestation with increasing clarity.

It's not too late to set brand-new intentions for increase or attraction, as this is still a time of powerful potential. If you're timing your spells with the Moon's presence in the sky, work with the hours between midday to midnight.

GODDESSES: Athena (Greek), Bast (Egyptian), Rhiannon (Welsh)

Waxing Half to Full (Gibbous)

Shortly after reaching the half, or second-quarter mark, it becomes clear that the Moon is nearly full. People tend to notice the Moon more during this phase, as it emerges just after sunset and rises later into the night sky. Energies begin to intensify at this time, with heightened emotions and sharper instincts manifesting at the conscious level. Magical intentions set at the New Moon and tended throughout the waxing phase will show signs of coming into fruition, provided we continue to believe in our success. The Goddess is now coming into her Mother aspect, her womb growing larger as the Moon grows with each passing hour.

Magically, this is considered to be an "all-purpose" phase, but the work should still be focused on increase and drawing what you

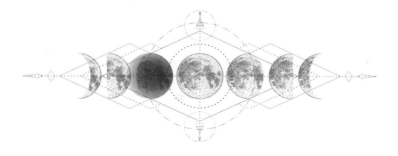

desire into your life. If you feel guided to do so, you may want to give a final boost of energy to any work begun at any point in the waxing phase. Also be sure to take time to note any progress that has become apparent so far, no matter how subtle. Give yourself a pat on the back for any and all actions you've taken in pursuit of your goal, regardless of whether they seem to have had any effect. Continue to pay attention to your dreams and your intuitive hunches for messages you may be receiving from the Universe related to your desires.

As for new intentions, the waxing gibbous Moon has a "quickening" energy to it, so spells cast now will manifest swiftly, particularly if they are simple and well focused. This energy is best harnessed after sundown and before the first stirrings of dawn.

GODDESSES: Nuit (Egyptian), Asteria (Greek), Luna (Roman).

The Full Moon

The Full Moon is the most powerful phase of the entire lunar cycle. Even people who don't believe in magic are able to recognize that something is energetically "different" at the Full Moon, as they experience strong emotions, come across erratic behavior in themselves or others, or face strange sleep patterns. Those who do understand magic are in an excellent position to take advantage of these lunar energies and bring their desires into physical reality at this time. The Mother aspect of the Triple Goddess is in her full power now, lending her nurturing and tending energies to our manifestations in progress.

Many Witches find that the day of the Full Moon is the most magically potent day of the month, making it an excellent time for Esbat rituals. Magic related to particularly important goals is

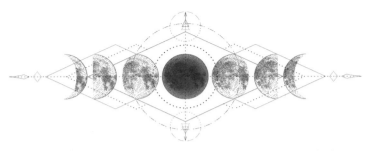

often worked at this time. Divination can also be particularly successful now, as can efforts to improve psychic abilities. Any and all magical purposes are favored at the Full Moon.

Many also make a point of expressing gratitude in their Esbat celebrations. You may wish to write a list of all that has benefited you over the past month and express your appreciation for these blessings. Doing so before making any new magical requests is a great way to both honor abundance, a theme of the Full Moon, and raise your vibrational frequency to an optimal state before sending out your new intention.

As for the intentions with which you began this lunar cycle, use this phase to acknowledge once again the progress made thus far, to clarify what it is you want to see happen next, and to realign yourself with the energies of accomplishing your goal. Often, the cocreative nature of manifestation means that you may experience a "false start" or two, which helps you refine your vision of what is ultimately the best outcome. For example, maybe you landed an interview for a job, only to discover that the company is not a good fit for you. You can use this experience to help you visualize, to an even more specific degree, the career circumstances that will suit you best.

As with the New Moon, many Witches try to work as closely as possible to the exact moment that the Moon becomes full for maximum magical advantage. However, this moment often occurs at midday or early in the morning, which can be inconvenient, especially for covens holding an Esbat. Since working under moonlight is also an ideal condition for magic, it can be just as effective to cast your spells several hours later, once the sun has set and the Moon has risen, or else the night before it turns full.

Although many agree that it's better to work before the Moon turns full than afterward, what you choose to do is entirely up to your degree of focused intention and your circumstances. There may be situations when you just aren't able to time your work according to ideal conditions. Don't let that prevent you from celebrating the Full Moon and casting your spell with enthusiasm.

GODDESSES: All Mother goddesses, such as Arianrhod (Welsh), Danu (Irish), Isis (Egyptian), Selene (Greek)

Full to Waning Half (Gibbous)

Within a few days after the Full Moon, the strong lunar energies have begun to recede, ebbing like the ocean waves just after high tide. Now begins the waning half of the cycle, as the Moon starts to disappear gradually into shadow. The Mother Goddess has reached the point of full maturity along her path and now progresses onward to greater wisdom as she ages.

This is a time to harvest the fruit of our magical efforts, which includes affirming and giving thanks for any manifestations that have arrived or are on the horizon. Be sure to enjoy everything that has come into your life and celebrate your efforts on both the physical and nonphysical planes. This is also the time to release the energy of outward action and align yourself with the energy of inward reflection. Let go of any spellwork that has yet to come into fruition. This doesn't mean you should give up on your goals—just release any attachments you have to outcomes from this

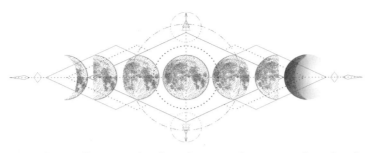

particular spell. It may be that there is a larger timeline for the manifestation to occur than you'd like, and you will need to have patience and trust in Universal timing. In the meantime, you can take advantage of the waning energies of the lunar cycle to make some beneficial changes in your life.

Eliminating negative energies and experiences is the governing principle of magic during the waning Moon. Spellwork aimed at overcoming obstacles, resolving conflicts, and removing causes of illness is favored now. Looking within and examining your inner landscape at this time can bring about clarity and help you identify where you can make more effective choices around recurring issues, both in your spellwork and in your daily life.

If you're still preoccupied by a goal that hasn't been realized during this time, shift your focus to one of banishing obstacles and releasing resistance—including any resistance to the fact that it hasn't yet manifested. Remember that you get what you focus on, so if you're having trouble envisioning your manifestation without feeling anxious or disappointed, work a spell for releasing those negative feelings and attachments. As the Moon wanes, the obstacles, problems, and negative thought patterns you're experiencing will also recede. As with the Full Moon, working magic at night when the Moon is visible is ideal.

GODDESSES: Demeter (Greek), Ceres (Roman), Freya (Norse)

Waning Half

Just as the waxing Half Moon is a time when the projective, active energies of growth ramp up, the waning Half Moon is accompanied by an amplification of the receptive, passive energies of release. The Moon rises later with each passing night, with less and less illumination.

Witches embrace both the light and the dark as equal parts of the whole of our experience on Earth. While the focus of your magic during the waning Half Moon may be on the less fun or joyful aspects of life, such as dealing with the unwanted or breaking unhealthy habits, we can appreciate the happiness that work will ultimately bring into our lives.

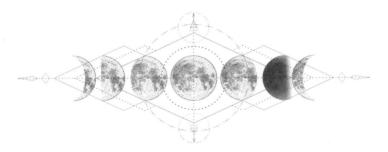

As mentioned above, spellwork during the waning Moon is aimed at banishing and releasing negative influences and circumstances. Depending on how you view your life, you may have a fairly long list of things that fall into these categories. For some, the process of deciding what to tackle at this time can feel overwhelming and even lead to despair, but there's no need to let the tricky work of addressing difficult issues get you down. For one thing, you're never expected to clear up all negativity from your life in one fell swoop! The work of removing what you don't want is similar to the work of attracting what you do want—your focus can't be on all things at the same time. Happily, there will always be another two weeks of waning lunar energy to harness during the Moon's next cycle.

You can make some wise decisions about your magical aims by taking one of the following approaches. First, is there anything going on with you that needs immediate attention, such as a case of the flu or a mechanical issue with your car? If so, the waning Half Moon is a perfect time to work a spell for releasing and resolving these problems. If there are no immediately pressing issues, then simply identify a goal that feels achievable to you at this time. Perhaps it's releasing an addictive relationship with a particular food or escaping unnecessary interactions with an annoying coworker.

For bigger, more challenging problems, it's advisable to wait until the Crescent or even Dark Moon to set your intentions. Many Witches find that the further the Moon wanes, the stronger its power to banish, remove, and release the unwanted. Use the first half of the waning phase for somewhat lighter work around release and removal, and draw on your successes to fuel your energy and confidence for the more powerful magic you want to work at the end of this lunar cycle. Night is still the best time for casting your spells, and you can still catch the Moon in the night sky for a few more evenings before it begins to rise quite late.

GODDESSES: The Cailleach (Celtic), Nepthys (Egyptian), Hella (Norse)

Waning Crescent

The waning Crescent Moon is the final point on the lunar cycle when the Moon is still visible. Energetically, this is a very powerful time for conquering negative circumstances through release and removal.

Magical work related to protection, banishing, and binding troublesome people or situations is favored now. However, be careful not to adopt an attitude of conflict or battle when it comes to the issues you're working to resolve. If you see yourself as being

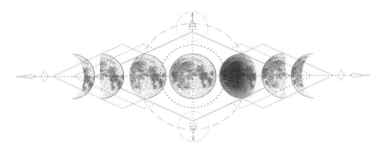

engaged in an active fight, you will most likely reinforce the negative conditions, rather than releasing them. For example, if your goal is to remove a major illness, keep your focus on how you will feel when you are well, rather than on "fighting" how you feel now. This is another instance where keeping the Law of Attraction in mind can really help you shape your magic. If you feel inclined, ask for assistance from the Crone Goddess, whose energies of wisdom and clear thinking are best suited for dealing with endings and removal.

For instance, if you're working to recover from a painful breakup of a romantic relationship, you might want to start with a spell to release your attachments to the past and then move to work related to healing the feelings that are hurting you right now. Don't put any energy into resentment about what happened or fear of what's coming next. Work for acceptance of things as they are, and know that this experience will help you to navigate the next relationship along your path. If you need to protect yourself from a person who is a harmful influence in your life, you can do a binding spell to keep them out of your way, but don't wish them harm in return. For one thing, this isn't necessary for your spellwork to succeed—in fact, negative intent will most likely lead your spell to backfire. When it comes to conflict of any kind, it's better to work for the best outcome for all involved, rather than trying to "win" or prove that you're right.

Waning magic is ideal to work at night, but timing to align with the Moon's presence in the sky is tricky since this Crescent won't rise until 3:00 a.m. That's a difficult time for most people to pull off any spellwork (but if you're able to, go for it)! If you're an early riser, you might try working just before dawn instead, as the Moon will still be climbing in the sky at that point.

GODDESSES: All Crone goddesses, such as Hecate (Greek), Cerridwen (Welsh), the Morrigan (Irish)

The Dark Moon

During the final stretch of days before the Moon turns New again, it cannot be seen at all in the sky. This is often experienced as a quiet yet strange time when energy levels fluctuate, logic becomes "fuzzy," and progress toward our goals can seem to be at a standstill.

This phase is also known as the "Balsamic Moon" in many traditions. The origins of the word *balsamic* are rooted in concepts related to healing, soothing, and restoring. Many Witches use this period in exactly this way, refraining from actively working magic while they relax and refresh their energy for the next waxing phase. This can be a time for reading up on new magical techniques and approaches as well as practicing divination and meditation. In some traditions, the Dark Moon is the ideal time for past life regression for the purpose of finding answers and insights regarding current challenges. Communicating with ancestors and loved ones in the spirit world can be especially productive during these days.

Abstaining from spellwork is certainly not mandatory. Plenty of people find the Dark Moon to be the best time for magic related to closure or bringing things full circle. We are still in the realm of the Crone, so this is a powerful time for releasing any karmic patterns that crop up again and again in your life, such as those related to lack, abandonment, betrayal, and more. There is a destructive potential to the energy now that can be harnessed for these purposes. As always, remember to focus your intent on eliminating the situation itself, rather than directing negativity at any people involved. If you're timing your magic with the Moon's presence in the sky (invisible though it may be), work spells between three in the morning and three in the afternoon. If you're having a difficult time for any reason during this phase, remember that the New Moon, and therefore a new beginning, is just around the corner.

GODDESSES: All Crone goddesses

A MISCELLANY OF MOON MAGIC

The final section of this guide is a short version of a "lunar" Book of Shadows. These spells, rituals, and magical crafts can be incorporated into Esbat celebrations or worked at any other point in the lunar cycle. You'll also find a useful chart for locating the Moon in the sky where you live and a table of spell ingredients that correspond powerfully with lunar energy.

A DAILY RITUAL FOR GREETING THE MOON

The best way to develop your own personal relationship with the Moon is to interact with it directly every day. Try integrating this brief ritual into your daily routine for the entirety of one lunar cycle. This is especially useful for those who are just starting to get acquainted with Moon magic, Wicca, or any other Nature-based spiritual path. It can take as little as two minutes, or longer if you like, depending on when you're able to work it into your schedule from day to day.

You will need to know when to expect the Moon to be visible in your area in order to plan. This information can easily be found online, and you can also refer to the rising and setting times chart at the end of part three for a rough guide.

For best results, stand outside under the Moon and gaze directly at it. If this isn't possible, look at it through a window. Truly look at it. See if you notice any new details about its exact shape, its shadowy features, its changing image as it disappears behind passing clouds and reemerges. If it's raining, you can still get a general sense of where the Moon is in the sky, so direct your focus there. If the Moon simply isn't in the sky at any point when you're awake, close your eyes and visualize it as it appears in its current phase and as clearly as you can. Spend some time silently communing with the lunar energy, and when you feel ready, say the following words (or compose your own). If you're unable to do the ritual privately, you can say them silently.

"Today/tonight I greet you, Moon, with joy.
Thank you for your divine light,
your Goddess energy,
your sacred power.
I open myself to your mysteries
and welcome your eternal wisdom.
So let it be."

Sit quietly for a moment or two, focusing on your breath, and take note of how the energy of this connection to lunar energy makes you feel.

FOUR QUARTERS MOON SPELL SERIES

This relatively simple spell is repeated throughout the lunar cycle, with variations appropriate to each phase. While each of the four spells can stand alone, there is a powerful advantage to working all of them in the same lunar cycle. Doing so will establish an energetic pattern that aligns you with the Moon's rhythms. You can tailor each working to your practice by stating your goals in your own words and by choosing your preferred combination of ingredients. Feel free to substitute any of the suggested items below with other Moon-associated crystals, herbs, and flowers. Each working might be focused on one aspect of the same goal, or the intentions for each spell may be unrelated to each other—it's all up to you.

≡ YOU WILL NEED ≡

1 work candle for atmosphere (optional)

3 small pieces of moonstone, smoky quartz, and/or quartz crystal

1 teaspoon dried hibiscus, anise seed, fresh or dried lilac petals,
dried Irish moss, or a combination of the above

1 white tea light or spell candle

≡ INSTRUCTIONS ≡

Light the work candle, if using. Arrange the crystals in a triangle shape around the spell candle, and then use the herbs and/or flowers to create a circle encompassing the triangle. Spend a few moments visualizing the Moon as it looks in its current phase. (You might want to place images of the Moon on your altar or workplace for help.) Now, visualize the outcome of manifesting your goal. When you feel ready, state your goal out loud, as if it has already come to be. Light the spell candle, and "seal the spell by saying the appropriate words below (or words of your own choosing):

For the first quarter (New Moon):

> *"For my intention I plant these seeds,*
> *knowing the Goddess will meet my needs."*

For the second quarter (Waxing Half):

> *"Day by day and night by night,*
> *my plans are growing with the light."*

For the third quarter (Full Moon):

> *"Abundant thanks for abundance blessed,*
> *and I know still more will manifest."*

For the fourth quarter (Waning Half):

> *"I now release this _____ unwanted,*
> *my mind is clear and my heart undaunted."*

Leave the candle to burn out on its own, under supervision. Spell candles will burn between 1–3 hours, while tea lights tend to last longer.

MAGICAL OIL BLENDS FOR LUNAR OCCASIONS

Anoint magical tools or wear a few drops of these blends during your spellwork on the New and Full Moons. Using pure essential oils, rather than synthetic fragrance oils, is strongly recommended. To avoid irritating your skin, be sure to use two tablespoons of carrier oil, such as almond, jojoba, or grapeseed oil, to dilute the essential oil blends before applying.

If you plan to wear an oil blend, it's wise to do a patch test first to make sure it won't irritate your skin and remember that citrus oils are photosensitive, **so avoid using lemon oil if it is exposed to sunlight.** (See page 78 for more information about conducting a patch test and photosensitive oils.) **Also note: this spell includes jasmine oil and clary sage oil; avoid using these when pregnant or breastfeeding.**

═ YOU WILL NEED ═

2 small mason jars (or other jar with a tight-fitting lid)
2 small dropper bottles for storing the blends (optional)

Full Moon Oil

4 drops jasmine essential oil

3 drops sandalwood essential oil

2 drops clary sage essential oil

New Moon Oil

3 drops lemon essential oil

2 drops rose essential oil

2 drops sandalwood essential oil

≡ INSTRUCTIONS ≡

Combine the essential oils for each blend in a mason jar. If you like, transfer the blends to small dropper bottles, which results in less oxidation over time. Blended oils will stay good for several months to one year, provided they're stored in a cool, dark place.

FULL MOON RITUAL BATH SALTS

Whether you're meeting up with like-minded Witches or celebrating solo, use this ritual bath to prepare for a powerful night of Full Moon magic. **Note: This spell includes mugwort leaves and lavender oil; avoid mugwort while pregnant or breastfeeding, and avoid lavender oil during the first trimester of pregnancy.**

≡ YOU WILL NEED ≡

3 tablespoons sea salt

¼ teaspoon dried hibiscus petals

¼ teaspoon dried mugwort leaves

⅛ teaspoon anise seed

2–3 drops lavender essential oil

Place the salt in a small bowl. Place the herbs in a mortar and pestle, and gently crush them while combining thoroughly. Pour them into the bowl with the salt and stir. Add the oil and stir again. Add to the bath while running the water. If your drain clogs easily, use a mesh strainer to catch the herbs when you're finished with your bath.

Spend some time reflecting on what you've manifested in your life in the past two weeks since the New Moon, and what intentions you'd like to set going forward. Also be sure to make a point of appreciating all that is working for you in your life, as this is a time to celebrate abundance and good fortune. When you're ready to exit the bath, take a few deep breaths and note the calm, centered state of mind you've achieved with this ritual. Keep this energy as you go about your evening.

Charging Tools with Lunar Energy

Of the many methods for infusing your ritual tools and spell ingredients with magical energy, charging them under the light of the Moon is one of the simplest and most effective. Moonlight is known to have both cleansing and charging properties, so you don't have to worry about clearing the old energy from your items as a separate step. For best results, leave your tools out overnight under the Full Moon, or at least in a windowsill where they will receive direct moonlight. Lunar energy is particularly suited to charging crystals and other mineral stones—particularly those associated with intuitive and psychic abilities. You can really see and feel the effect of the Moon on your crystals the next day—they'll be shiny and new and feel great in your hand!

MOON
≡ SPELL INGREDIENTS ≡

These are the most common colors, crystals, flowers, herbs, incense, and oils associated with the Moon. There are more of each, of course, across various Wiccan traditions, which you can find in your own explorations.

COLORS	CRYSTALS	FLOWERS	HERBS	INCENSE	OILS
SILVER	Moonstone	Hyacinth	Moonwort	Sandalwood	Lemon balm
WHITE	Pearl	Hibiscus	Mugwort	Myrrh	Jasmine
ROYAL BLUE	Smoky quartz	Lily	Fennel	Lavender	Sandalwood
INDIGO	Selenite	Lilac	Anise seed	White sage	Camphor
VIOLET	Quartz crystal	Iris	Evening primrose	Vervain	Rose
GRAY	Meteorite	Lotus	Irish moss	Jasmine	Clary sage

MOON
RISING AND SETTING TIMES

This very basic tracking tool will help you learn to find the Moon in the sky on a daily basis. You can search online for the exact rising and setting times for where you live online. Eventually, as you get into a practice of locating the Moon throughout the course of its cycle, you'll develop an instinctual feel for when to expect—and not to expect—the Moon to appear in your view of the sky.

MOON PHASE	MOONRISE	MOONSET
NEW	Sunrise	Sunset
FIRST QUARTER	Local noon	Local midnight
FULL	Sunset	Sunrise
THIRD QUARTER	Local midnight	Local noon

CONCLUSION

———

IDEALLY, NO MATTER WHAT FORM YOUR INDIVIDUAL SPIRI-
tual practice takes, the act of honoring and celebrating the
Wheel of the Year should be viewed as an art, rather than a rigid,
unchanging routine. After all, the days may be measured out by
clock and calendar, and the seasons may turn with a fair amount
of predictability, but no two days, weeks, or seasons are exactly
alike. This guide was written in that spirit, offering insight
and information that will hopefully help you develop your own
unique relationship with the magic of the turning seasons and
the ever-shifting energies of the lunar cycle.

As you progress along your path from one season to the next,
the Sabbats provide regular opportunities to learn and grow
in your faith. The same is true of Esbats, whether you observe
the New Moon or Full Moon (or both!) each month. Likewise,
each day provides you with an opportunity to take a moment to
connect with the God of the Sun and the Goddess of the Moon,
whether through a formal ritual or a brief, silent greeting.

As the years go by, the experience of "turning the Wheel" will
become richer and more rewarding. Indeed, the wise among us
say that you are never done learning, so by all means don't stop
here! As a next step in expanding your knowledge, you might
check out some of the resources listed on pages 156–157. And
no matter where you go from here, may the God and Goddess be
ever present with you on your path.

ACKNOWLEDGMENTS

As always, my deep appreciation extends to my birth family and my chosen family for their infinite love and support. Thanks to Ali Parker for witchy and writerly friendship. To Claudia Schmidt for her inspiring words about much maligned seasons. And to Denise, Shannon, and Dimita for living the magic in every moment.

Of course, enormous thanks to the team at Sterling! To Barbara Berger for her creative vision for this book, and to Elysia Liang for insightful edits. To Elizabeth Lindy for another beautiful cover design; creative director Jo Obarowski; Gina Bonanno and Sharon Jacobs for the beautiful interior design, direction, and layout; photo editor Linda Liang for sourcing the artwork in these pages; production editor Ellina Litmanovich; and production manager Ellen Day-Hudson.

SUGGESTIONS
FOR FURTHER READING

L IKE SO MUCH IN WICCA AND THE LARGER PAGAN WORLD, THE
Wheel of the Year is an enormous topic, with many variations
among traditions and individuals who celebrate the Sabbats.
Likewise, Moon magic is a vast realm that's always ripe for further exploration. This brief list of books offers some solid places
to expand your knowledge.

While you'll no doubt find some overlap of information among
these resources, each author brings their own individual experiences and perspective to the topics. It's always worth the effort
to learn as much as you can in order to deepen your own practice.
Happy reading!

Ahlquist, Diane. *Moon Spells: How to Use the Phases of the Moon to Get What You Want*. Avon, MA: Adams Media, 2002.

Boland, Yasmin. *Moonology: Working with the Magic of Lunar Cycles*. Carlsbad, CA: Hay House, 2016.

Budapest, Zsuzsanna E. *Grandmother Moon: Lunar Magic in Our Lives—Spells, Rituals, Goddesses, Legends, and Emotions Under the Moon*. San Francisco: HarperSanFrancisco, 1991.

Campanelli, Pauline. *Wheel of the Year: Living the Magical Life*. St. Paul, MN: Llewellyn, 1989.

Conway, D. J. *Moon Magick: Myth & Magic, Crafts & Recipes, Rituals & Spells*. St. Paul, MN: Llewellyn, 1995.

Holland, Eileen. *The Spellcaster's Reference: Magickal Timing for the Wheel of the Year.* Newburyport, MA: Wieser, 2009.

Kynes, Sandra. *A Year of Magic: Sabbats & Rituals for Solitaries & Covens.* St. Paul, MN: Llewellyn, 2004.

McCoy, Edain. *Sabbats: A Witch's Approach to Living the Old Ways.* St. Paul, MN: Llewellyn, 2002.

Morrison, Dorothy. *Everyday Moon Magic: Spells & Rituals for Abundant Living.* St. Paul, MN: Llewellyn, 2004.

Moura, Ann. *Mansions of the Moon for the Green Witch: A Complete Book of Lunar Magic.* Woodbury, MN: Llewellyn, 2010.

Nock, Judy Ann. *The Provenance Press Guide to the Wiccan Year: A Year Round Guide to Spells, Rituals, and Holiday Celebrations.* Avon, MA: Provenance Press, 2007.

Patterson, Rachel. *Moon Magic.* Alresford, Hants U.K.: Moon Books, 2014.

Pennick, Nigel. *The Pagan Book of Days: A Guide to the Festivals, Traditions, and Sacred Days of the Year.* Rochester, VT: Destiny Books, 2001.

INDEX

PICTURE CREDITS

ABOUT THE AUTHOR

LISA CHAMBERLAIN is the successful author of more than twenty books on Wicca, divination, and magical living, including *Wicca Candle Magic*, *Wicca Crystal Magic*, *Wicca Herbal Magic*, *Wicca Book of Spells*, *Wicca for Beginners*, *Runes for Beginners*, and *Magic and the Law of Attraction*. As an intuitive empath, she has been exploring Wicca, magic, and other esoteric traditions since her teenage years. Her spiritual journey has included a traditional solitary Wiccan practice as well as more eclectic studies across a wide range of belief systems. Lisa's focus is on positive magic that promotes self-empowerment for the good of the whole.

You can find out more about her and her work at her website, wiccaliving.com.